Praise for *One Out of Two*

"Sada writes with genuine amusement and a conversational ease."

—*Publishers Weekly*

"There is humor, pathos, and social commentary running through the lines and pages of Sada's clever piece, and whether you have a twin, know twins, wish you were a twin, or any other sibling desire or experience, this novel will both entertain and disconcert you."

—*World Literature Today*

"Singular, colorful. . . . With Joycean turns of phrase, humor, and a sometimes dizzying pace, Sada follows the sisters as they attempt to do with the suitor what they've always done: share. For fans of succinct, clever fiction."

—*Booklist*

"[Sada's] winding, lyrical, frequently abstract language is one of the great joys of this comical, silly and touching story. . . . Sada dances his reader through these conflicts and on to a joyfully droll and loving conclusion. His playfulness with language, plot and character make *One Out of Two* a true pleasure."

—*Shelf Awareness*

"A poignant farce in which surreal touches are infused into seemingly everyday moments. . . . A delicious romp of a novel."

—*Pasatiempo*

"Beautifully rendered in Katherine Silver's translation, Sada's prose has a unique rhythm and is spry and wiry, leading the reader into unexpected philosophical ruminating that is laced with dry wit and playful humour."

—*PopMatters*

"Silver has taken care to give us a sense of the original's idiosyncratic flavor. . . . [*One Out of Two* is] both a ribald rom-com and, at the same time, a sober and astute commentary on the inexorability of patriarchy."

—*The Scofield*

"From the dream team behind *Almost Never* (Graywolf, 2012), giant of Latin American literature Daniel Sada and acclaimed translator Katherine Silver, this compact hundred-page book is tightly stitched with the same perfectionism as its twin heroines' tailoring output. On the surface, it is a delightful romp to be devoured in one sitting, but linger longer with the text and it raises profound questions about the desire for union with another person versus personal independence."

—*Three Percent*

"Thanks to Sada's controlled artistry and Katherine Silver's sparkling translation, [*One Out of Two*] manages to enchant and amuse. . . . This entertaining romp is all the more intriguing for the way it follows a familiar template while doing something refreshingly new."

—*Star Tribune*

ONE OUT OF TWO

Daniel Sada

Translated from the Spanish by **Katherine Silver**

SPEAKING TIGER

SPEAKING TIGER PUBLISHING PVT. LTD
4381/4 Ansari Road, Daryaganj,
New Delhi–110002, India

Originally published in Spanish, with the title *Una de dos*,
by Tusquets Editores, Barcelona, Spain.
Published by arrangement with Graywolf Press, Minneapolis,
United State of America.

First published in English in the United States by Graywolf Press 2015
First published in India in paperback by Speaking Tiger 2017

ISBN: 978-93-86702-02-9
eISBN: 978-93-86702-18-0

10 9 8 7 6 5 4 3 2 1

For sale in South Asia only

Printed at Sanat Printers, Kundli

For Adriana Jiménez, my wife;
for Fernanda, our daughter.

Because he who loves
knows not what he loves
nor why he loves
nor what love is

—Alberto Caeiro

ONE OUT OF TWO

Now, how to say it? One out of two, or two in one, or what? The Gamal sisters were identical. To say, as people do, "They were like two peas in a pod," the same age, the same height, and wearing, by choice, the same hairdo. Moreover, they both must have weighed around 130 pounds—let's move into the present—: that is, from a certain distance: which is which? One is the other, and the other sometimes denies it, though always secretly, of course, because this business of having a double can be vexatious, almost *almost* leech-like, but it's their own fault, because with each passing year they try ever harder to emulate each other. Their tics, gestures, and facial expressions, all the same, as if mirror images. Do they ever grow weary of one another? . . . Possibly, though if they did, their souls would be void. The thing is: their sole importance has only ever been this similitude—a double meaning that just might be single.

On the other hand: there are differences in the details. Constitución Gamal has a sizable beauty mark just above her right shoulder blade, whereas the other doesn't: her name is Gloria and she is the more subdued of the two, the observer, so . . . This physical trait is easy to conceal: they wear clothes that cover that particular zone. For their daily attire: in the morning, whoever gets to it first decides for both, chooses the style and color, and the other simply consents . . . There's no discussion, no sudden whims.

As for their personalities: one is discreet and the other a chatterbox, but this, too, can be managed: neither indulges excessively, as a rule. And their names? They swap them—why shouldn't they! Their daily duties: they are seamstresses, and such perfectionists . . . Paltry, dullards.

What began as an innocuous pastime became the profession that took hold.

Many years ago they set up shop here: in Ocampo: where they live without so much as a twinge of longing, confident that their daily and incessant toil will yield wonders, that good fortune is bound to result from great effort, that good fortune is a star unseen by any eye: all of these, safe deductions they have both pondered deeply. Very *very* deeply! The twins could even be considered prosperous, if by prosperity we mean never aspiring to more than a local outing, and if making do with little is a boon, so—let's toast! because from time to time they celebrate their glorious life, at night they play records and dance. They get drunk: two, even three glasses each, when the next day is Saturday or Sunday.

They sew all their own clothes, empathically, logically, to avoid eccentricities that wouldn't suit them anyway—their fabrics are all bargain basement—and their Singer pedal sewing machines are the mobile symbols of their inventiveness. The possibility that these machines might articulate delicacy, beauty, and intelligence remains a fantasy: unfounded. The strength of their legs also plays a part, strength that seems to be on the wane, because our twins: well, they don't feel over the hill, but their faces—let's just say, if they didn't apply creams and lotions night and day, they'd look the worse for wear, though, from up close, that is . . . In spite of being forty, they still look exactly alike.

"One little slip, and you could be Gloria, and I, Constitución."

"So what? Maybe we'd both come out ahead," the other says sardonically, not believing a word of it.

"That means that old age might finally free us. We'll have to learn about very sophisticated diets and ways of applying makeup, otherwise it'll be really hard to stay the same."

"But we aren't old; forty years is nothing when there's faith."

"If God made us identical, he's not going to play some dirty trick on us now that we're all grown up," she who is supposedly the most taciturn persuasively asserts.

"You're right. People still can't tell us apart from a distance, or even from up close . . . though not *that* up close."

"Exactly, we'll always be identical, you'll see. We shouldn't give up now," came next, then: Gloria, with charming malice, lifts her finger as high as it can go, and Constitución imitates her with mirth. They're both pretty dotty, and they'd love to start jumping around like a pair of rambunctious teens. But, standing there face-to-face, they feel ashamed for having spoken like that, and they return to their machines with their heads bowed.

These kinds of exchanges don't carry much weight because there's so much history between them, because their identity has been a long and difficult compromise, minute by minute and day by day forging them into one accidental and unambiguous joint spirit. One can almost say that the Gamal sisters are saints: a single pureness.

Hence, their repartee has always served to boost their flagging spirits and help them decide together what to do. That's why the smart-alecky sassiness exhibited moments ago is a sure sign of senile bitterness, even if they do refuse to admit to it . . . And now let's turn back to the past, a serene past until the following occurred: they were still young, around thirteen years old, and the only children of parents who often went away, when these perished in a highway accident. On that occasion, the Gamal sisters had been left alone, by parental edict, to reign over their home in Lamadrid—nor was this the first time—with no servants, neighbors, or friends to check in on them; this fact, alone, sheds light on the family's social problems. Gloria and Constitución dealt with their seclusion by merrily sharing their daily chores. In fact, they never left the house, not even for a breath of fresh air, even though they could: why should they, for heaven's sake! Moreover, their parents didn't leave them a single peso, though they had enough provisions to last approximately two weeks.

Truth be told, the girls never wondered why their parents didn't consider taking them along on their extended jaunts, but this solitude both imposed and shared was a lasso of sorts that their Lord or their future, or maybe even the Devil, had tossed to them. Those days spent on their own were grand days of apprenticeship: a flourishing sisterhood coming into its own right: because they invented games till they grew drowsy, cooked up all kinds of dishes, and talked about what they would do when they grew up. On that particular occasion, at least at first, they delighted in their parents' prolonged absence, but . . . to put it in other words: one week: fine; two weeks: who cares! But by the third: what's going on here?: their distress was subtly gathering steam. By the fourth week, the twins began to feel pangs from the lack of food, and even worse, the total absence of news.

The parents' punishment for leaving their daughters in the lurch came abruptly: they got totaled! Soledad Guadarrama, their aunt from Nadadores, found the famished girls curled up in bed: cowering under the blankets. Without a second thought, she went straight to the nearest store and returned with pounds of meat and medicinal salves to revive them. A miracle was wrought . . . after which, with a minimum of tact, she told them the naked truth:

"Your parents were killed in a highway accident. Apparently, it was horrible; according to the report, their heads got severed, but they were identified anyway. The only solace I can offer you: your dead parents were given a Christian burial in the Múzquiz cemetery."

"Why did they bury them there, so far away?" asked the chatterbox.

"Well, probably because that's where the accident happened. The highway authorities gave the order to bury all of them in a pile in a huge pit, and on top they planted a cross for each of the dead, their names written in big white letters so if family members want to claim a corpse, men will come with picks and shovels and identify them, then they can take them wherever they want."

"They buried them without coffins?" asked the quiet one.

"So it seems . . . "

Why ask more questions? A dreadful silence ensued. They all caught a glimpse of the gloomy image of filing such a claim, so the girls, not to mention the aunt, never mentioned the subject again . . . It would be so irksome . . . The mere thought of seeing their loved ones stiff and decayed and having to bring them all the way to Lamadrid silenced them. They kept to themselves any impulse to act.

Though this deliberate repression made sprout within

each a seedling of guilt that would with time grow and become conscious. Let us, however, stay put in the moment:

"What I want to tell you is that I've decided what we're going to do: the two of you will come with me to Nadadores. You'll live with us until you get married. You'll have to do some kind of work and find a husband fast, or, if you choose to be spinsters, you'll have to save enough money so that you can eventually be independent. I won't ask you for a single peso from your earnings, I'll leave that up to you, and the reason I'm taking you with me is that it's a way I can return all the favors your parents did for me. As for the house: we'll put it up for sale today, so: go pack your things and we'll lock it up! I promise to give you the money from the sale, minus a small percentage as a fee for carrying out the transaction. So, let's go!"

The Gamal sisters, like two broad-tailed doves, listened to their aunt's reckoning; from them: nary a peep, alive but dumbstruck statues. Resigned and poker-faced: what choice did they have? They understood that despite the tragedy, the news had come to them via their most beloved and indulgent aunt, the only person who thought the two of them extraordinary, the person who had visited them most since they were born. She adored them: she made the FOR SALE sign with ineffable care, and hung it on the door, and . . .

Let's move swiftly to Nadadores, to their new and now bustling life wholly devoid of any thrills or sense of fulfillment; their dear aunt was mother to eleven: mostly brats; her husband: a plump grocer who smoked and always went shirtless, carried an air of uncertainty, and indulged in extravagantly long naps. The quarters assigned to the twins were cramped. They slept in a small room with seven of the other children, who pulled their hair and lifted their dresses. Unbearable. But, because it was a favor, the girls didn't dare complain.

Since they were still adolescents, the image of this period can be described in simple terms: someone is trying to reach for something high up and gets annoyed because she doesn't think to remove the blindfold that's preventing her from seeing, moreover: why should she? Still, she stretches, she gropes, she sets her sights on beauty, longs for it. But in this case, no; Gloria and Constitución developed in the opposite direction: cute little girls, though not even that, and unsightly young women. All that's left from the difficult years they spent in Nadadores is a fairly rotten stigma.

Stretching and groping, that's all.

Fantasies destined to develop only so far lest they provoke the most mundane of fears. The time they spent in that town could be summed up in three words: "They found work." They learned to sew in a small garment factory: yes: there was skill and there was excellence, but never originality, working only from premade patterns, complying only to others' tastes, without any personal flair; their compensation was a comfortable salary and defective minds. Alas, if only deep down they harbored a few superficial ideas, but not even there. What young women they were! And old ladies, as well!

Locked in their daily drudgery and vain alienation, locked in a plausible equilibrium; to bear up because one must and bemoan one's fate in silence, sullying the soul. But: it had to happen: a door finally opened a crack. Several years later, when they were already legal adults, they decided to escape from that gouged labyrinth; they'd known for a long time that the house in Lamadrid had been sold, but Soledad Guadarrama, maybe a miser and maybe a crook, had held on to their share. One rainy night—at the dinner table while eating scrambled eggs with onion and garlic—between ahems and ahas and a few dodgy turns of phrase, she told them about the transaction:

"Someone else now owns your house; I made a good sale, and here's my plan: I'll give you your money when you come of age. Until then, assume you have nothing. It's my moral duty not to give any of it to you now."

And her excuse stretched on: she plumped it up with opportunistic themes, while, under the table, each counted on her fingers the years and months that had to pass before she'd have her share. Only Constitución had the wherewithal to ask for clarification:

"But you're definitely going to give it to us, right?"

"Of course. What, do you think I'm a scoundrel? I always go to Mass, and I pray a lot."

"How much is there?" Gloria asked.

The husband, and uncle, but only by name: a huisache bush, far *far* away, without a say and never in the way, smoothed down his mustache: here was his chance to make himself scarce. The children scurried off to bed. Alone, the three women turned to the serious matter at hand. The breakthrough scenario: a bare bulb overhead—incubus—in otherwise shadowy surroundings. With sober self-importance, Soledad pulled out a pencil and paper; she could, if she wanted to, fiddle with the numbers, but those few extra bills would be like poisoned darts in her heart.

Hence, in the act, the magic of numbers pulsated. Division and subtraction, the rule of threes, and: the phantom sum shimmered when named, turning into an object of longing because it was so wholly unsuspected. Like a tree of possibilities. Dreaming of the future through long and sleepless nights, so long, in fact, that they sometimes nodded off at work; their output as seamstresses decreased, and that's why they made an enormous effort—the unwholesome athleticism of maintaining a more or less cheerful countenance in the bosom of that large family, especially while also: working brutally long hours—and recovered their determination, aware that their imagination had cut them off from the world. For two long years, until they reached adulthood, they were stuck, as the saying goes, between a rock and a hard place. A margin not worth remembering. One day they would flee, but with dignity. The time finally came for the transfer of funds and some decisions.

"We want to leave."

"But . . ."

"We want to live on our own. Give us our share of the money . . . And, yes, we are grateful to you for everything."

"Can I at least know where you're going?"

"Not too far, but to a different town," Gloria replied immediately.

"For heaven's sake, just tell me where!"

"No, we won't," Constitución cried out. "Didn't you hear, not far? Somewhere in the desert, yes, where it's hot."

Sacramento, Castaños, Cuatro Ciénegas, or a bit beyond: Australia and Finisterre, et cetera: which one? The aunt, after shuffling through names and guessing wrong, said, now finally resigned:

"Okay, I understand, but you must never forget that we're family. I'm here for you, whether you need me or not; come visit us whenever you want. I'll send you off with one final piece of advice: get married soon and have loads of children! Children are life's gift to women. Without any more fuss, I'll ask one small favor: send me your address so I can write to you!"

Soledad went straight to the mattress under which she'd stashed the plastic-wrapped sum of miraculous proportions. She handed them each a wad of bills, tried to act aloof, but then cried and brought her hands to her face with the utmost humility. The twins, indifferent, set about counting the bills. Once tallied: done: a large sum, everything they needed to make a real go of it, especially when combined with their savings, accumulated in dribs and drabs.

"I'm going to say it again: get married."

How could they ever get married when they spent all their time together?

Which would he pick? To feed both—now there's a thought—with luscious bodies, but their faces: better to keep lips sealed: that's what a possible suitor would most likely think . . . They were, are, good women, singularly talented and well educated, but you couldn't tell as much by looking at them. This is where desire comes into play: it's possible that someone someday would win their hearts: one as opposed to the other: interesting because: "to each her own . . .": indeed. Things get more complicated when we remember that because of their rare curse—having been marked before they were born by the hand of God or the Devil—the ingrates looked more and more alike as the years went by: a genuine conjugation, and apparently unavoidable. But, fortunate? Hmm . . . Next, they took the necessary step: to pack their suitcases. Two each, neither too heavy. No possession is worth much when there is so much money to spend.

Now for their send-off. Hands waving: farewell! in front of the house, like an embossment of such deep relief it perforates the page: the aunt, the shirtless smoking husband, and around them: the urchins, holding still: their mischief kept under wraps; they would have loved to run after the twins and lift up their skirts one last time, so they'd never forget their innocent pranks.

But there is restraint and irritability, if you will: ephemeral sorrows: yes: that seem to complement each other; there are: knots in throats that are easy to untangle and eyes staring long and hard in this direction: at the girls, who turn to look back out of a sense of duty, to express their gratitude with subtle effusion. Farewell . . . oh, dear! Then, they turn to face forward and catch a glimpse of a blurry figure that has yet to take shape; but sorrowful departures must not be prolonged or repeated, because saying goodbye more than once, according to a local superstition, is like spilling salt, or even like returning whence one hailed, because all paths are erased once taken. A curtain is drawn and behind it an improbable space opens up and . . . No. The Gamal twins sped up their steps: identical strands of hair blown in the breeze. To tell the truth: they were not heading anywhere in particular, at least not in spirit.

/

Pedaling—in the present—to the rhythm of a song: there's always something, here in Ocampo, for these machines that are almost human to do: their clientele has grown and will continue to do so if they keep at it . . . These days Constitución and Gloria think complacently of their humble beginnings. What a difficult position to take off from! Here: they've been settled for ten years after wandering from place to place looking for just the right conditions. Ocampo is it and will continue to be for as long as things go well.

Now let's tell their tale: after they learned to work morning, noon, and night, their ambitions became so thoroughly sealed by the absolute value they placed on money that one peso poorly spent, they feared, would ruin them. With this as their guiding principle, they sustained the flow, and despite constant increases in costs and prices, it never devolved to a trickle. They never went under because they had learned their fundamental lesson: to live without luxuries.

Except—for to be miserly is also to err—they dipped into their capital to buy a portable black-and-white camera. It was very important that the pictures they took be true to their similitude: to prove it, constantly, but no, not even this was enough.

On the contrary, each revelation fused them more fully together: grimaces of hilarity and grimaces of gravity: one out of two or two in one or . . . Pretending they were poor was an affirming and robust lesson that stripped them of all incident and regret, and from such a tender age to eagerly envisage their endless toil at tailoring and dressmaking, see it with lyrical eyes and absorb it into their spirits, know that they might fall headlong into an absurd abyss if they strayed even a little—that's what they gleaned from such dogged dedication.

In the meantime, they remained single—what of it? Enviable privilege and great courage were required to counter the advice of their aunt, with whom they kept in touch via exceedingly concise missives; from time to time Gloria sent photos and the other sent others: all against a backdrop of desolate desert landscapes and adobe walls: they sent them out of a sense of duty, and the response was always the same—arriving with alacrity wherever they were living: "Get married, you silly girls, and be quick about it! But don't flirt with the first young man you meet; you have to be coy, give yourselves airs, or you'll regret it . . ." They opened the envelopes together and with delectable malice. What mirrored mirth! So much reiteration was like a riddle without enough clues, an agonizing idea that never breaks through its own closed sphere.

But if we wished to draw conclusions, we'd be wrong to assert that they dug in their heels. Nothing of the sort! . . . "Better alone than in bad company" is a well-known expression they heard all too often throughout their long and arduous wanderings, and living without a husband's agreeable ways made them feel more fulfilled . . . Sacrifice and faith: this is what they learned from remaining in their immaculate state, no matter where they happened to be, and the rewards of motherhood would come later.

Their eyes never strayed from their goal: not even a peek at that wad of bills, for caprice too often trumps reason—yes, indeed! they knew this all too well—and they found work in a variety of places to pursue their larger purpose of becoming accomplished seamstresses, earning humiliating salaries in exchange for learning those sundry skills. Luck was on their side, even in this, for every town and every village needs somebody to make clothes. They became so proficient, whether sewing by machine or by hand, that they were able to formulate a theory. This, then, is the principle:

"The secret is in the needle after the scissors have made their cut." And a long explanation follows.

One was the other's teacher and the other also had to be hers. Their nighttime conversations, accompanied by romantic music and generous libations, usually turned on the conundrum of velocity versus perfection: which?: one has to be better, but according to what or to whom?

At that point, they really did have to think about their future. That's why they looked at the stash still packed away in that plastic bag Soledad had given them . . . The truth is, they hesitated, but . . . They considered Ocampo, a peaceful town with friendly people, and found plenty of reasons to test their luck there.

They made their decision one bright, sunny day: to go there right away and invest most of their inheritance. Nearly sight unseen, they bought a not very big house with a rather rustic patio; they also bought a couple of used sewing machines: Singer, top of the line, as well as a spot to set up their new shop. They doled out money for furniture, necessities, knickknacks, making purchases here and there and . . . Finally, all of it: the whole story in Lamadrid, their parents' horrendous accident and—to top it off—profane burial, then their life in Nadadores, their setbacks, their recoveries, at some point all got spirited away: cruel memories: except Soledad, their legendary aunt whom they never visited because they didn't want to quarrel, for by now they were in their thirties and had their own opinions, though they appreciated her for her honesty, for having helped them get on their feet: but not for her own self, not for her company.

"We have to write to our aunt."

"You're right, we should tell her where we're living."

Time passed: one day, under their front door: the twins

found a large, lovely orange envelope. It was undoubtedly a letter from . . . They opened it and read: "You're invited to the wedding of my son, Benigno; my boy is getting married. Both of you should come, we're throwing a big shindig. I suggest you do your hair differently: for example, one could wear it down, and the other, piled on top of her head in a tower. And don't dress the same, and don't stick together the whole time. Take my advice. There'll be many single men and you might just catch one. No matter what, I'm sending you my blessings, and remember, we always have a big bed for you in my house, because: things are better around here, not like before, now we even have enough money to travel. Anyway, it would be our pleasure to welcome you into our home again. Fondly, your aunt who misses you, Soledad Guadarrama." The date of the wedding was written along the bottom of the blue card, especially for them . . . In four days' time.

At this point—we should get our bearings—the Gamal sisters were rapidly approaching their forty-second birthday. Across their foreheads and under their eyes, down their necks and along their eyelids, clear ridges had appeared, as if some phantom fiend visited them at night and sculpted their slumbering countenances, and while they were at it, their bodies, with the clear intention of making them look more alike: making them one—poor things—: as if life were pure and vain idealism, for the number two can never be one. Whatever the case, and as for their sameness, we could wax eloquent, speak of dimensions and analogous depths, but . . .

Constitución and Gloria found in that invitation—by all measures, kind—the key to their perhaps most deeply buried preoccupation: "There'll be many single men." Such crass nonsense because: after reading this refrain, the twins saw each other and themselves differently, and from that moment on the ambiguous gift of looking so much alike began to make them uncomfortable. They could not both go to Nadadores.

No matter how badly they now wanted to look different, even with makeup, each on her own: without agreeing or intentionally seeking obvious contrasts: no: their identity was fixed, it was a curse and that was the end of it and nobody knows why. That is: in the past they'd tried: if one dolled herself up, the other wouldn't; if one wore a dress, the other would put on trousers . . . But folks aren't so easily fooled: even if they managed it in Sacramento or Cuatro Ciénegas, or even here, in Ocampo: they were recognized: on the bus, but more to the point: their luck in love was limited to much-too-furtive glances: from the absentminded. Which is precisely why they never went to dance parties: moreover, they were so unsightly that nobody ever chose them, not even the drunks. Hence, their path was narrow and grew ever narrower as the years went by . . . What horrors! a knife's edge, a distant glint, and maybe unnecessary.

Then that wedding: an opportunity, an illusion, a short vacation, a break from the routine, even if this marvel of meticulousness was a source of pleasure. Which is why they didn't have the slightest remorse about being slackers because from seven in the morning till seven at night—twelve full hours of toil, well, except an hour and a half to rest, figured into the schedule and offering concrete benefits, lest we think otherwise: the midday meal, washing up then lying down on different beds: sleeping soundly for fifteen or maybe ten minutes: power naps—every day except Sunday their customers arrived with their fabrics and left satisfied, their garments packed in bags with handles—paper bags—that the twins used because they happened to like them. Though lately, they had so many people traipsing through their door that they were falling behind, so rather than fail to fill orders as promised, they sewed till midnight almost every day. Hence, the stress previously mentioned.

Hence, also, the success—they worked for cheap—that allowed them to forget for long stretches their lack of acquiescence to love: men and their kisses, the sexual divide, those ecstatic shapes of bodies intertwined: over there, in the impossible beyond: tenderness was there, in the heavens.

That's why this was so disruptive. The wedding. The separation. The attempt to find out if somehow: the gnosis of a miracle: a suitor might unexpectedly appear. But only one would go, because both, they couldn't, no way. They discussed it extensively, the pros and the cons . . .

And they finally decide who would go to Nadadores with the flip of a coin. Heads or tails? Constitución won, and poor Gloria: she was left in a terrible predicament! She'd have to work double. One could even say, she'd have to work fast—chuck the usual perfectionism—if she was going to keep up with the orders. For her to fully embrace her defeat would require a change in criteria. To cleanse herself of envy so as to condescend, pretend to be someone who cared, though to tell the truth, deep down she bitterly wished that the other had been the one who'd lost, even if she was her equal. They still looked alike, but Gloria wanted to deny it when tails turned up and her ire rose.

"I hope you find someone good: a real man; but don't get your hopes up too high."

Wary dismay, and ultimately: razor-sharp envy; the loser issued her warning in tremulous tones and under the guise of great sincerity as she sewed without looking at her dear sister's girlish delight, the perspicacious or deeply wise winner knowing how imprudent it would be to say anything that might provoke a silly spat, that it was advisable, for now, to accept the advice, pretending to repress her sense of triumph.

"You're right, I shouldn't get my hopes up too high."

The talkative one, however, was a hypocrite, for she rose at dawn, in the dark and stealthily, not making any noise that would rouse she who remained unconscious. Complicated maneuvers to dress: then running euphorically the four blocks to the shop, after leaving on the bed a short note that read: "I'll be at the shop. I'm going to make a dress out of our finest fabric, because I'm thrilled to be going to Nadadores. This is, after all, my big chance." These lines, when read by the other, made her think that a fundamental attitudinal change had been wrought. What the devil had Constitución dreamed?

Erroneous notions. Getting all in a tizzy over a make-believe affection.

Now the gloating had come out in the open and was on the verge of flooding the scene or creating total disarray, as if the winning twin wished to provoke, or so the defeated sister saw it, heavy-duty envy or cold indifference or—why else? And that cursed coin toss now loomed large and powerful enough to destroy her twin. Imminent danger of . . . Gloria thought to herself: "I don't like the look of things . . . I'm going to the shop. I'm going to set that girl straight."

And off she went without even a bite of breakfast. Also running . . . There Constitución was, nose to grindstone, sewing her dress, her attention so rapt that she failed to notice the other's noisy arrival, until that one said:

"I can't envy you because what is yours is mine and vice versa. Isn't that what we agreed years ago? What? Aren't we exactly alike? I don't understand why you came here so early, almost *almost* sneaking out. I didn't care for your note. What's wrong with you? Who do you think you are? What's gotten into you?"

To which the other replied, "You're right, I shouldn't get my hopes up too high."

"Don't play that part with me. You're all in a tizzy over something you have no idea about, and I don't want you coming back sad if you don't get what you want."

"You're right, I shouldn't get my hopes up too high."

Stubborn as a mule—a hypocrite and a fool—she kept sewing, not paying any attention to the irate protestations of the loser. That same sentence, "You're right . . ." et cetera: repeated over and over, as if it were the only thought in her head. And dawn broke and the other—the roles reversed: therefore—expressed her rage till she had nothing left but regret: while Constitución was, as it were, borne aloft by longing: the taste of dripping honey, the slow probing, or the words whispered into her ear by the man of her dreams. Scents and lingering gazes! Sinking gently. Kissing.

In the wake of her foolish outburst, Gloria turned tender. She couldn't figure out how to look good in the far-gone eyes of her sister, who kept pounding away at the pedal: if she docilely repeated that same meek and innocent sentence, it's because she didn't want to gloat over her triumph, which also explains the extent of her conscious restraint.

"Forgive me, sister dearest . . . I do wish you all the best: I want you to have the most wonderful time ever. I know that all your pleasures and rejoicings will also be mine."

Herewith a scene of relative closure, each with her own notions looking for subterfuges, paths that would lead them to the core of their own pet daydream, or to a false principle, wherever the power of suggestion reigns.

The interim. Working like rodents, for it was silence that held sway.

All the while, customers came and left, gracious and grateful, like an apocryphal procession of manikins and marionettes. The shop: the setting, and the sisters, each in her own way, pondering separations as well as surprising alliances. About the wedding: say no more; about the toss of the coin: not that either; about luck: maybe . . . Throughout these fateful days: they ate, they worked very hard in complete silence. Words: only those that were absolutely essential. There was one sentence—at night: just before bed, here's what Gloria said:

"I hope you come back with good news; I'm going to sleep peacefully, for what is yours is mine, as you well know."

Full stop, next scene, the day of reckoning.

Constitución left. Her sister stood at the door to the shop and raised her hand to bid farewell. There is always a first time. Always a tearing, loose threads dangling . . . But Gloria remained stubborn:

"Have a great time and say hi to everybody for me, I hope you bring back—"

She didn't finish because her sister quickly placed distance between them: such a small and indifferent figure she made. Only an indistinct echo remained in the air. Then: intimacy as an idea that unravels.

Here, her equal, the part that didn't go: no tears or futile stratagems, no mannerisms, only the closing of ranks and strong convictions. And a quick return to take a look around the work space: a concrete desert filled with squalor and lacking air. Nascent longing and the word *absence* seeping into the sewing machines.

Chin up! for it's ten o'clock in the morning and a workday, and no matter what, the customers keep placing more orders, paying down a deposit or the whole amount up front.

The unfilled orders. So much to do, and along came someone who asked the inevitable, "Where's your sister?" and the response was necessarily friendly though laced with a certain trace of evasiveness. Many other such questions ensued, which she answered between clenched teeth. The barrage of interrogations let up only in the afternoon when Gloria closed the door and continued pedaling till midnight. Alone, self-contained, restrained.

The action started just as her fatigue set in, at bedtime. She imagined the shindig, the enveloping music, and her sister sitting on a chair, alone, silent, a woodpecker perched on a branch, a toy bird, poised and waiting for a polite man of reasonable height to ask her to dance, but not even the midgets bothered. Lying in bed, Gloria conjured that sad scene, suffered in her own flesh the moment her aunt approached to try to coax her out, lead her enthusiastically over to the heart of the wedding party: the young newlyweds mingling, the toasts, the *Cheers!* Where everyone was milling. Where shoulders were rubbed and introductions made . . .

That opportunity, that moment, aah . . . Gloria closed her eyes and drifted off to sleep. Inside, in her mind, there was a series of reversals, furtive exchanges, evocative stencils of bodies in full abandon. Then, as things unfolded, improbable shapes arose out of somewhere: soft and gentle nakedness . . .

Untethered, floating, alone and bewildered. Then the couplings: in a blue space, Gloria kissing an otherworldly man, surrendering fully to the initiative his hands and tongue were taking, while her twin staggered around with mouth agape, unable to get anywhere near no matter how hard she tried. Yes, then a sequel with a smoky hue, a pursuit, and proximity: melting into an illusive silhouette of passion and desire: hence, only a tiny taste of satisfaction. Insinuations of such vast pleasure! How unattainable, though, for both of them!

/

Welcome to the wedding . . . What a lovely dress! Why didn't the other one come? Yes, I understand, now you'll have a better chance of finding a man. Best thing to do is just smile, at everybody . . .

/

Handshakes fade. Dance steps and glasses breaking. Swirls of laughter and dropped words. It smells like alcohol, meat, a little bit of a lot of things . . . Swoons, faces, blurry figures, and her aunt keeping an eagle eye out . . . from the shadows, at a certain distance, because that's how it should be done . . .

/

It all started up again the morning her sister bustled into Ocampo: her hair down and her silhouette suddenly framed in the doorway of the shop. Gloria, to avoid an effusive greeting, pretended not to see her, sat steadfastly at her machine, the pedal going below, focused on the next stitch and the one after that; she probably had a good excuse, or—how to put it?—was formulating one.

She had the habit, as did the other, of keeping her eyes on her work except when a customer spoke to her; a quirk like that can be advantageous, and that goes for both of them, because losing one's concentration under those circumstances could even cause an accident. Knowing this, her sister didn't say a word, preferring to approach quietly, so she removed her high-heeled shoes and left her bag where it was. Once in front of the other, she uttered her best sentence ever:

"I danced all night with a slender man of interesting age."

At that, the loser, both incredulous and wary, looked up. Eyes meet by way of divination, and embarrassment: eyes no longer identical: not now: then a tremulous lapse that seemed to last too long; the one sitting down now more tentative, and the one with her hair down, racier. But Gloria laughed as if the dance didn't matter at all, for according to her, it was nothing but a trap, though in fact: a spiteful and invidious guffaw, that then ended: when:

"He's coming to the shop next Sunday; I gave him this address. The plan is to go for a stroll. I think I'll take him to the walnut grove at the edge of town."

For a brief instant Gloria wanted to remind her of their agreement, about how what was yours was mine and vice versa, but then she thought it better to listen, knowing that one had to be astute when it came to affairs of the heart: or, as ranchers say, sneaky as a snake. The other, in the meantime, was excited, and with her sister's implicit permission told the whole story from beginning to end. The encounter, the wedding as setting.

A bold exchange of glances that insinuates restiveness and invites approach, sweet words in short supply: from one to the other and back again in a move to tantalize, to kiss: why not? Though in this case: wait! for Constitución, based on her aunt's advice, it was important to first learn something about the man's background and social standing.

Along those same lines: let the suitor's true intentions come to light over time. Considering her age and considering her other baggage, she shouldn't go losing her head over some momentary fling.

So, hands were not held or fondled, except while dancing with the music swirling around them . . . And the dialogue flowed, two silhouettes and an affectionate mood, a future pointing who knows where.

For a moment, let us imagine—we must—the atmosphere and the rhythm framing the action, the magnetism between them: flirtatious Constitución dimly illuminated and wearing a lovely dress with a definite girlish touch. Let us imagine the man when his eyes lit upon her, dumbstruck at the sight of such a marvel, then, instinctively, with no introduction save a fixed stare, the culminating moment, the propitious sensation shared from afar, and the pull to connect.

Their faces said *yes:* ardor.

Everything necessary to start the ball rolling.

That tall man with pointy sideburns—and clearly descended from heaven—is thirty-five years old. A little younger than she, manageable: especially: because of the unpleasant tension of enduring a long and rocky bachelorhood. An exceedingly agreeable man who wears cowboy boots and a wide-brimmed hat, a country saint who smiles at the ladies while smoothing down his mustache to give himself airs. By no means, though, is he a popinjay. Just talk to him, and you'll see. He uses stratagems to make conquests, like any man at a dance. So much for his bearing, and as for what he does for a living: he buys and sells animals on credit or with cash. Only goats and pigs, because he doesn't yet own even a jalopy, so he transports his beasts strapped to the gratings on the roofs of the rundown trucks of strangers. Even so: he's doing just fine, thank you very much, and one day in the not-too-distant future he hopes to be the proud owner of a stakebed truck that he can use to transport his own livestock.

She dotted every *i* and crossed every *t* that had anything to do with her suitor, whose name was Oscar Segura. His likes, his dislikes, she was frank to a fault. Constitución even found out his real address—Calle Gómez Farías, number twenty-five, Colonia Zaragoza, Ciudad Frontera—which she corroborated with Soledad, as well as his marital status, just in case. In spite of his age, he lives with his parents and all his siblings. He is the eldest, and really as wonderful as they come, a paragon of good behavior, according to their aunt's account, with a warm heart and no attachments, so a great help to his parents in many important ways. A man of deep feeling without streaks of knavery or traces of cynicism. Quite the opposite: moral and generous, a fighting angel.

The winning twin gave a too-smug description of his upright figure, replete with details that were mostly beside the point. Carried away, she even said it would be her privilege to sketch him, especially his face, and she promptly picked up a nearby pencil and piece of paper. Though now an objection was raised:

"There's really no need, I can picture him just fine from your words," says the loser.

Then, to avoid any more of her sister's braggadocio, she stands up, like a spoiled child, or something of the sort: setting aside the tasks at hand, she walks over to the shop door. How puzzling.

There, sullen and fuming, she stands with her arms crossed. Staring off into the distance, or pretending to.

There is bitterness, there is pain, there is displeasure and probably injustice, for one was the spitting image of the other and now because of the toss of a coin, they no longer are. The so-called silent one never could have imagined that the Fates of love would show up after they'd been separated for only a few days. Herein, then, lies the catch, for an identical destiny would have been hers had that coin landed after one more turn.

Constitución watched her with surprise and, yes, at the same time placed a pencil behind her ear, like a carpenter . . . What had come over her equal? She finally understood that it might indeed have been a mistake to go on and on for so long and in so much boring detail simply because she was happy to have been noticed by a man, that is, any man, who was looking for a woman in order to . . . Because until then—and here's the truth—not even a horse had allowed his gaze to linger longingly on either of them, and it was for this very reason that Gloria could not be her accomplice either in this or in any other idyll. But the chatterbox refused to emulate her sister's angry attitude, and instead turned back to her work, telling herself: "I understand her anger, but I know she'll get over it. Anyway, she should be happy for me."

In the meantime, their customers came pouring in. As a rule, the twins didn't talk to anybody: they didn't like wasting time; they even put up a sign that read: WE ARE BUSY PROFESSIONALS. RESTRICT YOUR CONVERSATION TO THE BUSINESS AT HAND. PLEASE DO NOT DISTURB US FOR NO REASON. SINCERELY: THE GAMAL SISTERS. They did not want, of course, to be rude. For although the twins knew from experience that people take advantage of the least sign of friendliness to engage in endless gossip, they couldn't dispense with the politeness they had always shown between them. They had never shouted at each other like Furies, and they weren't about to start now.

Hence, in front of others, all that turbulence and subconscious delight got redirected back into their hearts, or their backbones, for they were women of integrity, even in the toughest of times, and they had to feign at least tainted harmony and elegance in front of others, show those who patronized their shop the concrete courtesies they deserved. Their success was—and they knew this—in large part built upon such a foundation.

Quick, even if nervous, dispatchers, with the requisite professional grins, because otherwise . . . Let's not forget that the competition is always lying in wait.

But, alas, this time wasn't like other times. The man from the wedding turned out to be a thunderbolt sundering them apart. The mere fact that he existed led to a still indecipherable double entendre. As soon as the customers left, they sulkily returned to their former positions: Gloria, by the door: stubborn; and the other hard at work, having forgotten, on top of everything else, to take the pencil out from behind her ear.

For a few brief moments, they looked like two withered chestnuts, the comings and goings of their customers preventing further developments. During one of these intervals, when they'd been left on their own, Gloria offered a solution:

"I'm going home, because I feel like it and because I think I've earned it, and I'm leaving the rest for you. Anyway, I don't need to ask your permission. While you were at the wedding, I worked myself to the bone, till midnight. I sewed more than twice as much. Now it's your turn . . . I'll see you there at lunchtime. I feel like making a delicious salad for the two of us."

There was a tug on her voice at the end: that "for the two of us," weighed down with surly sarcasm. The quiet one was finally and ardently showing her mettle. Constitución felt the hatchet fall gently, calmly, but also effectively.

And the loser, the one with right on her side, the one who wanted to complain without going too far, just far enough so that the other didn't dare reproach her, fled, because: a single nasty comment could be catastrophic. Let her go, what harm could it do? she wouldn't go far. Home, lunch. An understandable outrage: good grief!

Then came the moment when they were both sitting at the table sharing the culinary masterpiece that Gloria had prepared with incomparable care: a sumptuous salad of fresh produce, and myrtle juice, and some local ham bought who knows where. Lip-smacking! all this to stop the other from daring to question her attitude: those crossed arms and that knitted brow in the shop. She probably intuited that questions would carry more poison than salve; but, in spite of it all, what was extraordinary was not the clever gimmicks the winning twin used to make her case, but rather the diligence, the scrupulous and obvious artistry the loser had employed when laying out the meal.

The meanings, the feelings . . .

No.

Not a significant word passed between them. Constitución noticed a certain amount of envy being suppressed with great effort by she who had been, till then, her mirror. Envy? she thought, though maybe not: for there were no dramatic outpourings or angry pleas. So, what was going on? Throughout the meal, only the clinking of cutlery and a masquerade of good manners, no furtive glances sneaking out of the corner of an eye . . . Specifically, prudence held sway: still: she who had won had no choice but to keep a lid on it, think things through carefully. Gloria was the first to finish and, without even saying "excuse me," made quickly off to the bedroom. Such childish antics notwithstanding, the moment to clear the air had still not arrived, and, what else could the other do!: she chose to wait: whatever would be, would be, if, that is, it could be . . .

A tragedy or a joke?

What follows is as limpid as the light of day. Gloria went to bed: irresponsible. She who had always been so very obliging—in other words, a robot who sewed—was not that way today, not at all. Maybe sleep would spur her on the next day, but for now she willingly turned the reins of the shop over to her sister, who went straight there, leaving the issues they'd avoided all day to be broached after dark. There in the shop she could spin her own threads of action; in the meantime, she told herself: "I know, she's suffering, but I'd rather talk to her when she's more relaxed."

Constitución, all alone and with the shop door closed, stayed late elaborating shapes, but only of thought; she didn't work, either, not knowing for sure what she should do: merrily set about sewing as usual, and if so, what stitch should she use?: and how?; apply her scissors to an idea or the fabric itself?: such foolproof opposites, so which way to turn?: toward the vanity of having been chosen by a man who was, at least, well scrubbed, or toward the marvel or misfortune of that unavoidable likeness, her sister?: mirror, shadow, paradox, or diabolical curse; if she was fundamentally an obstacle . . . She made as if to do so—there was a lot of work—then stopped. Better for now to focus on the ordering of reality, one more day without stitching wouldn't provoke a sudden plunge, though . . . An idea crossed her mind that had come to seem more and more plausible over the past three months or so.

This was it: to let her hair grow so she could tease it into a beehive; and to wear different clothes than Gloria: garments that would reveal that enormous beauty mark above her right shoulder blade. Yes, so Oscar would see it right off the bat. Wear dark glasses and a darker shade of lipstick, or pencil her eyebrows, or . . .

Turning it over: her thoughts churning, and right around midnight, just as she was about to reach a decision, that is:

go to her sister to explain her resolve, a doubt suddenly appeared. The fact was, the two of them had been entwined since they were inside their mother's belly, and they had worked so hard to live life simply, as two peas in a pod. Two halves that had always been a single seed, a single pureness, and a single path. No, they couldn't separate, and a change at this stage, what would that entail? Constitución had to immediately repent, even feel ashamed. She couldn't bear for the other to suffer.

Detour—and an affirmation—back to feelings of sameness. Place herself on the other side of the mirror and from there understand, feel what the loser is now feeling. Better like this. As if some demon had sent her an urgent message from a primordial cave to make her mend her ways. How very amenable of him. And then there appeared, it had to appear, a pleasant temptation, the idea of sharing what she had with so much pluck acquired, then accepting the consequences. Once and for all, and just because, may the miracle fully embrace them both.

She bolted out of the shop. First, she put the padlock on the door, though she forgot to switch off all the lights. She didn't realize this lapse would raise suspicions, for instance, like about how maybe those gals were so swamped with work that twenty-four hours weren't enough; how they'll go blind, even hunchbacked from sitting such long hours and focusing on all those knotty threads. Possible, but at that time of night, the lights were on at their house as well. What for?

So much light and sadness. Light! in a different sense: unanticipated luck. Constitución came bearing good news while the other was playing with beans—dry beans, even a little shriveled around the edges, just so you don't picture a mushy mess—killing idle hours and also reenacting them: according to her bitter understanding, her hands on the tablecloth: a bit disconcerted, no, very much so, because to tell the truth, sleepless Gloria was thinking about things related to separation, and if she shed a tear, it shined brightly then fell. Her fervor burned inwardly, but the winning twin, no matter how delectable she now felt herself to be, could not fail to notice the situation: her equal's sorry posture, hence the moment for:

"I thought you'd be asleep, you don't usually busy yourself with beans at this time of night. Well . . . I know what's bothering you, but I have a solution that'll cheer you up . . . "

And she spelled out the plan she had cooked up only a few minutes before, in short: "share the man," easy enough to say but the game would have to be played with strict rules that would, well . . . Consequences—what about them? Back to basics, which seen from the outside seemed ridiculous, that is, "emotional." The so-called lucky one summed up by proclaiming:

"You know that there's something mysterious that connects us and can't be broken. If God made us identical, it must have been for a good reason."

"But you—"

"There are no sensible *buts* about it, the only thing to say is that what's mine is yours and that's all there is to it."

The other one's face lit up.

Gloria! She, her very own self! She also made for love, for gripping sensual pastimes . . . and excess! And sighs! Everything she'd never hoped for, because: she'd already descried the rupture as she moved the beans around: what a paradox. And they embraced, just like that, as if by embracing they could merge into a single solitary spirit. It was time for a toast.

So: they took out the bottle of Club 45, full of enough booze to get them both quite tipsy.

Cheers! they said, and toasted to their good fortune, to perennial sisterhood, and yes: to be as they were, reluctantly submitting to but nonetheless taking a stand against love's conventions, against the relativity of the flesh, both of theirs, their parallel excitement, so that by clinking their glasses together they were marking the beginning of an enterprise that might very well compensate them for all their sorrows. And they played their records and danced with winged steps, and after they'd gotten thoroughly soused—gulp!—they discussed the precautions they would take, and between gales of laughter, they proposed guidelines: sustainable or not: but festive nonetheless, for tomorrow there'd be time for revisions.

In the meantime, wear beautiful dresses made with all the art their hands could muster. Not for anything in the whole wide world allow Oscar Segura, confident and enamored, to tempt them with pretty words, subtly, to shed their sexual modesty, not because the prospect of such delights disgusted them—not on your life!—but only to prevent rash actions of any kind, for therein lay the risk: if they undressed, he'd discover the birthmark that distinguished them. By the same token, they wouldn't be able to wear see-through clothes, or clothes for hot spells that leave the thighs and shoulders exposed, for that would cause insoluble problems. Most importantly, they would both go by the name "Constitución," so imagine the likeness; the same hairdo, the same tone of voice, to a highly nuanced degree, the same sweetness, intentionally, similar facial expressions and reactions—this, of course, not something they needed to rehearse—and as for what was discussed, they would tell each other immediately, almost word for word, so as to avoid blunders that would make Oscar suspect that he was dealing with two rather than one: an ideal one: the one and only apple of his eye.

Between toasts and off-the-cuff jokes, they came to agreement on many things . . . Constitución put down the stakes and the other followed the path laid out, without asides or any picking of nits, everything in proper order, and long like a river, very long . . .

Their dancing brought an end to their conversation, and they finally slumped over, their heads resting on the dining room table. Almost at dawn: total surrender.

They didn't give a hoot about missing a day of work: what the hell! The moment they were living demanded dissipation. But they did agree that the first date would go to the vanquisher, of course . . . As to the rest: the unfilled orders, the pushy customers, the shop left with the lights on, but closed. How did that happen? For how long? A whole day! . . . Two would have been better.

To wit: let people think whatever the hell they like.

/

"Look, there he is, three blocks away."

"Where?"

"That man, there, he's carrying something white with what looks like a red splotch on top."

"The one dressed in green?"

"Yes, he's stopping people, probably asking them where

the shop is, can you see? He's coming this way and . . . See how long his strides are?"

"Not bad-looking . . . Though . . . "

"Hey, what's up with you? Remember what we agreed? Go, hide, and step on it!"

"But, it's just . . . There's nowhere *to* hide, and I can't just crouch down in the corner."

"Put on a hat and get out of here. He mustn't see you."

"What hat? Don't tell me you want me to put on that orange one?"

"I don't care what you put on, even a scrap of fabric to cover your head, but go, run, run. Now!"

Gloria did as she was told, placed two or three rags over her head, and with another she covered her face but left one eye exposed; with the rush and her nerves, she almost stumbled but righted herself unscathed, then scurried away in the opposite direction from Oscar, who was but a few steps away, yes, just as Constitución was becoming overeager—her plan was to act cool rather than bold, so she stood smugly to one side of the shop door, pretending to seem interesting by staring off into the distance; in the meantime, the other, forcibly sent on her way, looked like a bizarre lay sister of sorts, and once round the corner, she stopped and removed the rags. Some passersby must have witnessed that particular act, for it wasn't a sight one sees every day.

Sunday. The day for bathing and lavishly applying perfumes. In the evening, people go for a stroll to get some air, especially during those dog days of summer: out: to see and be seen, by inertia to the town square: the place for local beauties with salacious gaits. Lots of monkey business today, which is why some busybody would undoubtedly notice the morbid curiosity of that lady lurking on the corner, and farther away, the other supposedly aloof one standing at the shop door . . . and at her age? What a scenario! and the fact that one of them was hiding made it all so obvious. Everybody knew them!

From what Gloria could see, at the only moment she dared look, her victorious sister—be that as it may—talked to the man, then padlocked the shop door shut. First step accomplished; per their superpremeditated agreement, the suitor should never enter the shop, because if he saw the two machines, he'd start wheedling information out of them by asking lots of questions, and then some random detail, maybe circumstantial, would raise a doubt, possibly two; better not give him an inch: nothing: no way, never. The man had already handed her sister what he was carrying: a gift with a bow, which Constitución, certainly blushing, opened slowly: that is: without expressions of glee. All well and good. And, since today's watching twin knew that the lovebirds would go to the walnut grove on the edge of town: the edge was here: in this direction, they were coming her way, Gloria realized. So: rush away without losing sight of them. Now, more bereft then ever, because the unhappy spy had to quickly find a hiding place and cover her face again with those rags. No. Luckily she found a redoubt reserved especially for her, where she could watch them pass at a reasonable distance and where she could finally take a deep breath . . . A gift of fate . . . Then: follow them furtively like a black widow spider pressed against a wall: wherever, that is, there were walls.

Follow them: keeping those rags clutched firmly in her

hand in case the suitor turned around—she had to anticipate that—so she could quickly dissemble their too-obvious sameness. She continued, ever at the ready. That's how things transpired.

However, while they strolled, they still didn't touch—so much the better!—because desire sharpens, because a love like this, at least at first, seems very sacred. If only it could remain like that for a lifetime! . . . Though a little nibble, a tiny pinch of mischief, never goes begging.

Well, there was Constitución, her modesty fully intact.

In any case, they reached the spot: the glorious walnut grove, where huge logs lay thick and fallen: ideal and romantic: to sit down on one and from there contemplate the afternoon: alone: watching each other attentively, and those suggestive pauses, and Gloria observing that idyllic scene from afar, from behind a fir tree; she wanted to imagine the conversation, feel the same shivers her sister felt; that atmosphere imbued with voices wherein each word is a contour, and certain internal pressures are, might be, manifested in a nervous grimace or some chance brush of skin against skin. Herewith, the tragic struggle against temptation, the latent caresses, and the kisses that say so many things that cannot be expressed for the sake of simple equanimity, or rather: until things become a little clearer . . . Hands resting on the tree trunk, and that's all: perfectly still. Only approximations, where silence is: where silence would like to be a premise, maybe even nakedness, love, loyalty, substance: penetrating certainties: delayed passion.

His token of affection was a pair of bobble earrings, iridescent crystals for Gloria to wear because:

"He'll be back next Sunday. Now it's your turn, like we

agreed. But you should definitely wear these earrings," Constitución said.

More and more work, however, in the shop: they had to make up for lost time, otherwise their customers would take their business elsewhere. During that period, their competition was catching up, other shops were starting to open, though warily, not so much as to threaten their solvency, but, yes, at a certain point, enough for them to feel that they were not the only game in town.

After settling on their arrangement, which was good for both of them in the same way, and having left their turmoil behind, they were able to temper their emotions, and: their goals became once again what they had been: to be tops in their humble field: dullards, perfectionists, squeezing every last drop out of every hour of every day, as had always been their wont: morning, noon, and night, and making better use of their time by devoting themselves fully to their stitches and their dressmaking.

By keeping their eyes glued on that prize, they prevented people from tricking them into getting emotional over their still-budding courtship, or from the love of one affecting the other whereby both of them would end up leaving orders half done.

We repeat: if resentment ever popped up, it was by that time so well hidden, so puerile, and so spineless, it didn't matter a bit; in fact, neither made so much as a wisecrack, for they knew all too well that so much of what they were planning to live could never be anything more than a passionate game, a lurid possibility.

Nor—at least at first—did it cross their minds that a full experience of mutual love—without all that foolish tact—would end in tragedy. If both of them accepted the lie, an excess of fiction could possibly, ultimately, turn the mistake into a truth; a blind truth, but still; in other words—and this fits right in—they'd both marry him and have identical children and confusion would reign in spite of proper or bad manners, and taken even one step further: the government and the Church would, considering the circumstances, allow modern marriages between one man and two women or a girl and two or three boys . . . So, the attempt: would it be tragedy? comedy? drama? or what?

Supposition and faith complement each other. The etceteras are, will one day be, provisional certainties.

In other ways—it must be said—each continued to weave her own ideal. Such prerogatives, reconsidered by Gloria and concealed by Constitución, were avoided when they spoke. Calm and, indeed, industrious, they stuck to the grindstone, and when there weren't any customers, they took the opportunity to talk about the man, the ruse they were using, here and there dropping a hint or two about their doubts as to his intentions, satisfied, even in this, to pick apart the present and place it quickly on a sound footing.

Though . . .

Each coveted her own secrets, her own plans, just in case something unexpected occurred. In this case, Gloria, whose turn it was the following Sunday, wanted to be just a little bit treacherous: for: while listening every night to her sister's advice, she toyed with the possibility of playing something other than second fiddle in this relationship. She wanted, rather, to also take some initiative, though she never said as much, she only listened and acted the saint, as if not even butter would melt in her mouth. Two-faced! Yes, that's it, exactly the modifier she deserves. Especially when her sister mentioned such trifles as: that she shouldn't ask him about this, that, or the other because then Oscar would think that his charming girlfriend was forgetful, or even, God forbid, that she wasn't an ace with details, like so many other women around here.

At night, while they were dining on light fare—as they often did to watch their figures—Constitución, brimming with enthusiasm and verve, wanted to pick apart, point by point, the most salient features of her conversation so that the other wouldn't stick her foot in her mouth on the next date, and on Saturday night, the eve of, she took out a pencil and paper to write down step-by-step instructions: because she was nervous and for good reason.

With the morrow still hazy, the so-called chatterbox considered of utmost importance the suitor's concerns, a few of which we will mention in passing: he had a lot of questions about Constitución's background: What about her family? Where did her parents live? Where were they now? and without blinking an eye she told him that she had been orphaned when she was young and that her aunt from Nadadores had raised her until she became an adult: that she had left when she was around twenty or twenty-one. Saying it like that, with so much relative honesty, was to employ a feminine wile that allowed them to observe the candidate's reaction, though, to her relief, he said nothing that betrayed any shock, making only an expression of slight displeasure, superfluous if you wish, a not-very-sly wince that flitted across his face, no questions, as if to let her know that his love and devotion were of indisputable integrity.

Later, during that same loving exchange, he talked almost obsessively about his work, in other words: the weaning of she-goats and the difficulties involved in selling them; about how pigs were not very profitable. Out of all this, the real girlfriend conjured up abstract images that consisted of small arrows being shot at sentences—we could call them precepts—of the most profound transcendence.

"You don't need to be such a stickler. I promise you that when he gets here tomorrow, I'll be very cautious. I won't ask stupid questions or say anything compromising."

The other sighed passionately and mentioned in passing: "At the beginning, when we were alone there in the walnut grove, I could tell he wanted to kiss me on the cheek, or on the forehead, or who knows where; he sidled up close to me while I was gazing out over the horizon, acting like a donkey about to start braying; I: like a surly mare, turned quickly to face him and he politely backed off. It's better that way, not a good idea to give him too much leeway."

"No, not a good idea . . . but why?" Gloria asked herself, inside where her lewd plans were being laid.

Then came the long-awaited day and her opportunity. That first time . . .

The substitute was ready punctually at four in the afternoon, her hair done up in a do identical to her sister's, the same amount gathered and the same amount loose, flaunting those iridescent earrings: courtesy of the beau. The shop properly locked—to avoid any sudden urges—and at its door, the radiant figure Oscar took to be the same woman: without optical or other illusions; all of which Constitución watched from the street corner, as if she were a meddlesome child viewing romance from afar and longing to be there; others saw her, too: of course—Sunday, hot, vanities: imagine the pains they took, trying to guess since the week before which of the twins was dating.

Now he approaches, a bouquet of roses in hand, to walk again with his sweetheart to the walnut grove, after a flirtatious greeting; but then came an abrupt change, something not part of any plan: the loser brazenly sidled up to the rancher: who: he had no choice but to place his arm around her shoulder, hug her prettily and in the middle of the street: right there in plain view of the entire town: after which they continued on their way, pressed against each other while the other was pressing herself against walls: spidery: and from a distance also pressing her lips together and telling herself in a rage: "That blockhead already gave herself to him. I hope, at least, she keeps her virginity, that's the least she can do."

No way could she go yell at her; she had to bide and watch the scene scrupulously, follow them unflaggingly, because if her sister allowed him to grope her, so would she have to seven days hence and without any foolish haggling. To the chagrin of the observer, this Johnny-come-lately was painting the walls of her own scenario with wild and passionate hues splashed across the distance, cloud pompons dripping with ocher and deep red settling in between the hills. A perfect and unequaled backdrop for abandon, for those long, drawn-out kisses.

And: joy was had. Gloria and Oscar gave themselves to each other, surrendering to the undertow, their lips loose, large, labile: sudden soft and circular surfaces. Desire driving them on. Sitting on the tree trunk: Gloria let the man see the bouquet fall from her hands: intentionally and, what of it! she was spellbound. Triumphant or stupid. Over here, and on the other hand, the real sweetheart hiding behind a bush had to create her own illusions, as if she were experiencing in her own flesh that rancher's tongue thrust between her teeth. "Stop!" she well-nigh cried out instinctively, but her voice didn't carry, nothing was voiced. She thought about throwing a stick at them, forcing them to part, unlocking them from their bosom embrace, but from that distance she might fail to hit either on the back, or her missile might reach a bush, out of which would surely explode the ephemeral colors of many butterflies; so the poor thing gave up: resigned to her role that day: to watch with the composure of one who understands, or tries to.

Understand that her sister might be right, because if there rose between them a conflict over the man—a question of keeping a weather eye open—Gloria could boast that she had briefly but forevermore tasted affection, or at least amicable deception.

Anyway, Constitución walked away very carefully. She didn't want to see more, suffer in vain, ergo, the last scene she caught was a switch: they were conversing, sitting, almost motionless, holding hands: both in profile and between them, like an emblem, the hue of the evening as everlasting glue.

She left: the so-called winner had to go straight home. Furtively: hugging the walls? No need, considering the plenitude of the other two.

Next time . . . It would have to be like now: this was the lesson she had learned from her other half: no more imbecilic abstinence: instead: candid and open verve, though not allowing the man, in the pursuit of his traitorous and horny adventure, to touch a leg or a breast, neither under or over the clothes . . . Anyway, she had her doubts.

Lying there in bed, all alone, sunk in her uncertainties, she wanted her sister to get back already, not too late and not with her hair mussed from necking, that would be perdition, if . . . And as the minutes passed she pictured more and more excesses, or rather: the worst: that Gloria and Oscar had wandered to where the nopales grow, and that they hadn't gone sooner because they were waiting for it to grow dark; she even thought they might climb over a rise, there to give of themselves freely and lasciviously, away from the stares and the whispers, and so . . . Then, finally, while hanging from the heights of her tenterhooks, to her great relief she heard the creak of the front door.

It was Gloria, no doubt about it . . . Yes, indeed: who else could it be? Her other half, who found the house in shadows and silence, dreadful nightfall, though a sliver of light, like a tightrope, insinuated contours. It seemed as if the surroundings were turning sepia, as if plastered with peach marmalade, as she switched on light after light to look for her sister; as she made her way forward, intrigued, with the bouquet of flowers in her hand toward the bedroom the two of them shared; as she saw her twin under the covers—phew! at least she hadn't run off—with her eyes wide open, staring hard at her with a touch of terror in her pupils, or maybe intimidation; she didn't know whether to express her joy or ask if they were going to have dinner.

Cloaked madness and a static moment neither could intrude upon. Constitución did not want to demand an explanation for the kisses and touches, because the plan had been different, slower, more irksome. So they looked at each other, perplexed, as if good and evil had suddenly swapped places and from then on they could pretend to ignore both, maybe melt them down, or believe they had melted them down into a dreamy and detached state wherein nothing is truthful because it doesn't last long, because in the end it strays, because it fails to settle into a shape. And their stare is, their stares are, so many things. No . . . They must be simply fed up.

The prolonged stare they shared, eyes glued on eyes: one stare, one single unbreakable thought, bound together, therefore, also in the consequences. Stares that deliberate.

Static? . . . Who knows, because: the only thing Gloria wanted to do was give the flowers to her twin. It was an invitation to the continuation of an ideal: the other was grateful for her deference, so: the smooching sister timidly said:

"We can have fruit tonight if you'd like . . . "

Constitución jumped out of bed. Together but without touching, they made their way to the table.

"You, sit, I'll peel the mangoes and get them ready," Gloria said, trying to be very gentle.

Her twin consented—silent maneuvers—and: while they ate, their eyes suddenly met, not to hold the stare like before, instead, Constitución let slip a simple giggle, an emblematic trifle her twin did not know how to calibrate, and because it was so importune, seemed to her like mockery.

A mistake or fear or a tender swagger.

Which made Gloria grow sullen—pseudosentimental—anticipating rebukes and reprisals, and when she saw the other stanching her scorn, she took her revenge by smiling more broadly, as if to release some of her stress. Constitución's response was clear, petulant: she immediately let out a chortle, which led the other to follow with her own . . . A concert of crows . . . Finally, their nervousness found an outlet, hilarity was preferable to anger, at least it was more roguish.

The racket grew and grew . . .

Irrepressible, both . . . In the midst of their girlish guffawing, the painful narrative of their joyless lives played in their heads like a filmstrip of febrile images wherein their circumstances—piles of them—formed a vacuum, a vacuum that for better or for worse stood in counterpoint to what they never were nor ever would be: two different beings, two ideas, two premises in search of unity. So: they let themselves be carried off by a lyrical event; so: their laughter was their tears turned inside out by the terrible truth that they looked so much alike, that they could never ever be otherwise. Accursed roars of laughter that were soon heard in the street and perhaps—why ever not?—if their range was even wider, throughout the entire town.

Absolute proof to any passerby who heard that the love of one, or both for one, had driven them mad—rumors about their romance were spreading far and wide, and not in a good way—or that they were sloshed, though, who knows! . . . Likely speculations.

Then came the calm, as could be expected. Gloria was the first to force herself to quiet down, though the other was about to, as well. Oh, those eyes, they had to avert them if they wanted to prevent a second such remarkable outburst. Hence: they playacted, in a way; though this was not, not at all, their goal, these inane charades wouldn't last because before long they were once again sitting and facing each other like two mischievous girls, and:

Constitución pretending to be eyeing her plate full of uneaten mango: broke the ice by saying:

"I don't know if I saw right, I was far away and the sun was shining right in my face, but I did notice that you were really sidling up close to one another; what I mean is that we were brought up with principles, weren't we? Well, not to offend you, but I assume you didn't let him touch our noble parts."

Indeed, the loser had anticipated such a remark and responded like a daughter who was feeling contrite:

"The kisses and hugs you saw were the only ones."

"But that wasn't our plan. Why did you have to get so greedy?"

"So he won't forget you, so he'll stay up all night thinking of your love—" now with aplomb she confessed.

"It's just that—"

"Wait . . . I haven't finished . . . Look, I want to be completely honest. If I let him kiss me, as you saw, it was because I thought you might regret lending him to me, and I wanted to make the most of my opportunity, because I have no way of knowing if it'll be my last."

"Well, you shouldn't go around imagining things that aren't so. I would be incapable of betraying you, I honor our agreements."

"So do I, don't forget that I use your name and also don't forget that I lost the coin toss, and I didn't make a fuss when you went to the wedding."

"Yes, exactly, and I don't want to argue over stupid things, either. I don't like nasty jabs or backstabbing; we are above all that. What I'm worried about is that there's no going back now from your brashness. And I'll have to do what you did."

"Go right ahead, if you want to, that is. I highly recommend it. It's a way of keeping him hooked, at least in my opinion; you have to give him little bits at a time so he'll really fall in love, so he won't see you as some kind of archangel and give up; in short, so he'll always come back. What's more, you should remember that we aren't that young, and we're not gorgeous enough to be getting all persnickety."

"Maybe you're right . . . I wanted the romance to develop slowly, but we are getting on in years, and maybe we'll miss—"

"Exactly. What if on one of those many trips he takes he meets a beautiful young woman? Don't think it's not a possibility."

Bull's-eye. Paradox?: the loser won, the so-called quiet one scored lots of points. That view of things . . . —the result, it would seem, of surreptitious groping—was the balm that actually eased the qualms of the one who had won. It must now be said: in the meantime, this really was a game, or a strategy, devised by Gloria during those long stretches of restraint and strength of character, meant to place the other on the horns of a dilemma: to see whom the winner would choose at any given moment. It was about creating an insurmountable obstacle with the gentlest of means: still, deceptively dodgy: and totally overlooked, of course, why not? The real sweetheart wanted them to be reconciled because disputes always arise out of a lack of proportion, and her shaky idealism: puritanical, not even commonsensical: whereas the kissing twin was reevaluating their ruse, which placed their sisterhood on the highest pinnacle, though she didn't do it to frustrate in one fell swoop Constitución's illusions but rather to attenuate them, becloud at least slightly her jovial specter of the future.

The present: their eyes still locked, as if rummaging through in them for a simultaneous expression, which they found, finally, in a fresh though not deliberate smile.

Next: they got up to clear the table: sleepwalkers loath both to act and to resign themselves completely. Lights on: switch them off: night and irritability and the awareness that tomorrow is Monday and there are heaps of clothes in the shop: like pulling apart a colorful cake: work—and harmony and diligence and . . . —all of this remembered before falling asleep. To return to their credo of energetic principles. A difficult week awaited them: ugh: full of intense effort, and . . . Best to forget all about their obligations, because, anyway: it made more sense to go straight to sleep where their dreams could hold anything at all.

And the switcheroo: they had similar dreams: in black and white: flat, without pain or any emotion—they got out of bed very early and bathed, just like any other day: together: soaping each other—and once the cold water had revived their senses, they told each other: nothing: Oscar had vanished, though obviously they would remember him in their vigils, but, what a strange test for them! Then, identical preparations. Taking even more care with their lipstick and hair. Every single shining detail. Ready, set: which is which? Just as they were: they sat down at the table: a quick breakfast: a bite of whatever, then they were off.

A little before seven o'clock they opened the door of their shop. May the customers come, but those who did were not really customers but rather busybodies, and since the shop rarely opened so early, only a few straggled in, two by three, or one by one: stubborn early risers, just to confirm the rumors they'd heard: "Does one of you have a boyfriend?" "Congratulations!" "Brava!"; laughing to themselves: cynical. So annoying. Tightlipped: because the opinions of those inquiring were unwelcome. A boorish onslaught, but with a purpose. "How lucky you are! and at your age, it's not so easy to . . ." "I hope he has good manners!" "*He* does," was Constitución's cutting reply. Such comments are forbidden, and Gloria pointed with the longest needle she could find at the sign they had so recently hung up: . . . RESTRICT YOUR CONVERSATION TO THE BUSINESS AT HAND . . . SINCERELY: THE GAMAL SISTERS. The visitors were rendered speechless, the words balancing on the tips of their tongues, slippery or not, then scurried out the door with their tail between their legs. Stooges! But mostly: Deadbeats! The twins, then, wondered if it was better to keep their noses to the grindstone with the shop door shut so as not to have to dodge and duck all those people, so they could simply plug away—in blessed peace, we might say—with only the usual interruptions . . . Doubts lingered . . . but if they hung up said sign: on the door: outside: they would need to get a large nail and hammer it in hard, and, oh drat! what a waste of time! Moreover, truth be told: it would make them look far too stuck up. So . . .

Everything as it's always been and carry on. Fortunately, the higher the sun rose in the sky, the less besieged they were, and they didn't bother rehashing any of it with each other . . . what? As for the customers, the good ones, that is, those who knew the rules, one or another arrived every now and then, so the twins, in silence alone with each other, got a lot done.

Comments were still made, casually tossed off, by this person or that, while their garments were being handed to them and they paid: "You be very careful, now! That man might be a freeloader." Or: "So, when's the wedding?" Impossible to respond amicably, for their words sounded like jeers more than anything else. An "I don't know yet" from the real girlfriend would surely suffice, because people didn't insist; such a simple answer was all that was needed for a different and even more entertaining rumor to make its way through Ocampo.

The town was so small, so infernally small, that the gapers and eavesdroppers, though few in number, were already in hot pursuit.

You be very careful, now!

That imperative banged around in their brains because it was such excellent advice, whereas: they still hadn't given any thought to "the wedding," the date, and other such sacred problems, and although the twins did not talk, that is, during the days that preceded the following Sunday, the strain between them increased in tandem with all those nonsensical comments and the various directions, all clearly erroneous, they led to; meanwhile, the Gamals focused on the mountains of garments they needed to finish as well as new orders coming in, which, thank God, were not that complicated: cut to fit, that was the extent of it, with not very fine fabrics and no fancy finishings, their daily bread, ergo, they stayed up late working, wanting to recover in short order the prestige they had lost, according to their own deductions, as a result of their romance, and they deliberately left the shop door wide open so that people would see that they were still professionals, whether love was in their lives or not.

But every day and as if on purpose, the prattle and tittle-tattle reached their ears. Their customers continued to make crass comments that were, whether intended or not, insulting, like getting pecked at from behind and kept, as if, under siege—but: what choice did they have? A week of silences, to spite them, as if these martyred virgins were playing some kind of trick, though: at bedtime they deigned to acknowledge the gossipmongering, realizing that it was not in fact a good idea for one of them to spy on the other as they had been doing, it was only a matter of time before the gapers, as well as the giggling gaggle of kids, prying bandits that they were, who tailed whoever clung like a spider to the walls, would station themselves in different spots, near where the nopales grew so densely, along the green bank, to the south, to observe the openmouthed kisses Gloria or Constitución shared with her beau, and this would create an explosion: of enormous consequence.

To make matters worse, right around that time, on a Friday, a letter from their aunt was slipped under the door to their house: the old lady from Nadadores who'd been held in suspension, whom they'd thought dead, or something of the sort, or maybe just lazy or decrepit: somehow beyond hope, because she no longer wrote them weekly missives as had been her wont till then. So they tear open the envelope and see the shaky, not to say deathly ill, handwriting: *Girls, how have you been? I heard that one of you is going out with*—this part was illegible—*mna from gud ffamxili*—then things improved—*the best of Ciudad Frontera: the Seguras, because even though*—again, more gibberish from the scribbler—*they arnt vari reech the half vari gud manurs. Anyway*—this next part was very clear—*I don't know which of you it is. I beg you to tell me before I die, my rheumatism never gives me a moment's rest. I hope we hear wedding bells when we least expect them; let me know so I can come . . . Anyway, please tell me what's going on, and if you don't want to bother going to the post office to buy letter-sized envelopes and airmail stamps, as they now require, even though the letter will go by bus anyway, those shameless pencil pushers, if that's what's stopping you it would be easier for you to just come here and visit. Nadadores isn't so far away from Ocampo. I'm sure you could get here much faster than any letter you might write . . . And I want you to know that my husband and I would love to see you, I will personally cook you a delicious dinner . . . I hope*—here, again, more scribbles—*thither also haza bxyfrend . . . re mmbre is hurribl living witot ckildrn or witotha husband, watif sudnly one of u dize? txe othr*—followed by the really awful part despite the spelling and handwriting being impeccable—*who will still be in the land of the living, poor thing! she'll be left all alone and completely abandoned, and it'll be even worse if she's got some horrible disease, dear me! I can't stand even thinking about it. That's why I keep telling you what I've been telling you for as long as I've known you: Get married! Please! . . . Here at my house*—and the next sentence was impressive because clearly the aunt wanted to draw some very large and round letters—*EVERYBODY'S ALREADY GOTTEN MARRIED. I'M THE HAPPY GRANDMOTHER OF ELEVEN GRANDCHILDREN . . . YOUR AUNT WHO ALWAYS SUPPORTS YOU AND WANTS ONLY WHAT'S GOOD FOR YOU . . . P.S. DON'T FORGET TO WRITE BACK.*

After reading the letter, the twins stood perched like

two buzzards on the top of a tree, or rather: with the urge to fly away; in a game of sidelong glances, their crestfallen faces failed to find an appropriate expression. They could not, dared not, look at each other. The commotion in their minds was a shade of white and their ideas traced the cruel outline of a hateful outburst, because that sentence: "Everybody's already gotten married" . . . had to have been intended as either mockery or menace. Gloria, the one holding the piece of paper, bit her lip and seemed on the verge of collapse, but she managed to rein in her rage and: without asking permission from her other half, she furiously tore it up and hurled the tiny shreds into a nearby basket, while the other, without moving a single finger or saying anything about the other's rash act, observed her indulgently, trying to understand her motives, which were none other than her very own.

Shreds? Shards? Of the past? Of a bygone chapter . . . All up in smoke? . . . Yes, that's what they'd like, once and for all.

In response to the obvious insult, the shredding spoke volumes, a step forward, a proposal: to hell with the same old story: their aunt with her unrelenting advice, and the twins, considered spinsters, understood that this would be the last letter they would ever read, and if others arrived containing the same song and dance, as could only be expected—they imagined the handwriting even shakier, completely illegible—they would destroy them before opening. Moreover, why should they send pictures and greetings if the central topic was so obdurate and humiliating, if she treated them like dimwits? In addition, this business about her children getting married within such a short time—when were the weddings and when had

Soledad let them know?—was nothing but another form of pressure, a despicable lie, an obvious deception designed to propel them into action. Oh well, and still, each held on to her own secret and an event such as this was not about to make them reveal anything.

That's why they didn't speak, nor would they; instead, calmly and in spite of everything, they created some order out of all that psychological turmoil, because—knowing their own strengths, their impulses—the heated fluctuations of any discussion would expose the plans they each harbored regarding the beau. It can thereby be inferred that their future loomed, quite vague, and love: don't even mention that, though for now the only game they were playing was its pursuit and the emotions it wrought.

Around midnight, in their bedroom, they again looked at each other up close, the tips of their eagle-like noses almost *almost* touching. Their eyes revealed greater wisdom, a unique and sensible vulpinity. More united than ever?: finally, they embraced, for they would share the same fate. A discreet scene in which a single sentence was uttered for no particular purpose:

"I'm glad you tore up that hostile letter," Constitución said.

The bait was tempting, but Gloria, cleverly, was not about to start explaining her own reasoning: she offered only a blush: a touch of sadness, or to put it indirectly: she grinned like a Cheshire cat. With that, ipso facto, they released their tight embrace. The so-called winner made a hand signal, her fingers sticking out like horns that she moved in and out, flexing her fingers, her mouth keen, implausible thirst: her round lips moist, just look at them, will you!: she wanted to get tipsy, but her twin motioned no: wagging her index finger back and forth. Next came other gestures, hands moving every which way, grimaces, and even irony, they laughed and, what the hell!, because any subsequent disagreement would be the opposite of a celebration. Yes . . . Pantomimes and criteria that made it inappropriate to drink a toast right then—it was neither Friday nor Saturday—tomorrow they would have a lot of work, and . . . Alas, to sleep.

Chimera? Abyss? Each futile longing with its own *de motu* . . . The thing is, neither had the foggiest idea which single notion was indispensable for them to fully embark on a different life: with the burden of their similitude, still facing mirrors, but mirrors that are aging. As such, they seemed like two blind, even delirious women who find no walls or anything else worth groping . . . Only Oscar: with a stippled landscape behind him: for both of them: in one: dribbles and drabs . . . From afar, come here! Come now!, but no . . . The virtual sensation vanishes.

Dreams proliferate, come then go; days and duties—lapsing at night—: reality: just as it is: without ebb and flow; likewise the twins, making their usual sounds: grindstone and more grindstone, indeed: a monotony that seeks rootedness, a lethal pretense, or tentative beginnings, because: due to Oscar's punctual arrival every Sunday bearing gifts—bracelets, brooches, bobbles, and bottles of scent—they fell in love: in a similar way, even if deep down inside each was immersed in her own wiles: and: as time passed, that deeply perforated love couldn't be avoided but they couldn't talk about it, either, so in the end it would be an upheaval rather than an opportunity. By the same token, little by little such perfect presents gave the well-scrubbed beau partial license to kiss them gently, to lightly caress their knees, and thighs whenever possible—or rather, as far as the rancher was concerned, the pleasure was purely: his sweetheart sometimes yielding as she defended herself against his touches—so he, confident while riding those buses packed with passengers, could well imagine Constitución's legginess, and her sex further up—though he was decent: with self-control—: the possibility, whenever he thought about that triangle women have, where the young 'uns later come out, wow! though after all those feints and parries, the wedding would be a coronation, and after that, imagine the affection, the loving welcome when the husband arrives home weary from work and the gaggle of kids as well as his wife gather around him, large meals with proverbial seasonings prepared by his wife, years of the same life, serene: in short: he was savoring his own longing like wine that plumps up the senses before settling in for the long haul. But first, he'd have to knock himself out, fight and win many battles to earn his just reward.

The bad part is that those women were deceiving him, not out of treachery but rather sisterhood: that union so sanctioned that they never allowed themselves to be carried away by the fiddle of tickling fingers or a mouth that insinuates kisses, a current so strict that there's nothing to gain but restraint and a push to escape whenever it tries to extend its range, in itself a long, drawn-out game: serious later: and grand at the same time, because that blasted birthmark, if Oscar discovered it, you be very careful, and how! . . . In the meantime, the passage of his hands over the twins' skins should never include their backs or shoulders—no auxiliary hugs—so nothing but kisses and the real temptation: in between their thighs.

However, there are three mouths—more precisely, two: in one . . . And the other that accepts: three! and they talk, eat, and laugh, play at being the beginning of something that flows into: does silence hold more hope for happiness? These mouths—so sweet, so sisterly, then devilish, then saintly: transfigurations and time away from being either you or me; we: appearances, twins before all else, and then . . .

Grindstone and more grindstone, each one with her own credo, because Gloria, when she kissed her supposed boyfriend, would forget about her sister, thereby rendering the memory of those enchanted moments fodder for her dreams: same with the other, and for Oscar, of course. Whether eating, sleeping, or even while keeping their noses to it: many mental journeys.

And, of course, every time each went his or her own way, he or she carried a piece of the other. A triangle, to put it simply: three gnawed points and a conjugation: or to put it indirectly: two similar points and a third one far far away.

Passion conjugated: repressed, obsessive, in full conformity with the rules of the game; in fact, one could say that because there was so much uniformity in their actions—always stopping halfway—in all three of their igneous heads flowered a convulsive urge to tell all, but they had to wait.

However . . .

We must agree that between identical beings, mimicry also includes sanctuaries of sorrow that are impervious to being aired or traced, as well as very short-lived yet incommunicable points of view. Hence, after all those years they had learned to intuit each other from afar, to know without meaning to that they were being observed by the other. But, let's get to the point: currents ran between the Gamal sisters even when they were sleeping, yes, indeed, they were twins, to the *n*th degree, and proud of it, and here is one example:

Whenever one of them looked in the mirror for any length of time, for example, when she was getting all gussied up on Sunday, two hours or so before the beau arrived, the one looking would feel like it was her sister who was looking back at her out of that enormous and paradoxical full moon, intentionally imitating her primping, a form of mockery, and every once in a while—why not?—would quickly wink; then reality would return when her twin suddenly appeared beside her to hurry her along: because: with four of the same: oh, dear! which of them was who? If the reflection was accurate, they were all ghosts, or the other way around. Then, an outright denial when they left the gleaming, and the gleaming itself: would it flicker without them?

Also, in the shop or while eating lunch or dinner, when they were concentrating in total silence, one of them would suddenly say: "Don't worry about that. Oscar is dependable. He'll be back." To which the other, a bit taken aback yet pleased by the divination, in order to maintain the flow but not the sadness, would respond: "I'm so glad you think so, because sometimes I have my doubts. I don't know, maybe one day he'll regret our proper courtship." From there would ensue a conversation, which would then be abruptly cut off in order to tamp down their fears.

More recently, that is, when one Sunday followed another, they stopped spying on each other, only every once in a while, out of ghoulishness or avarice, but not systematically. Let's agree that for the one whose turn it wasn't, the best thing to do was get into bed and wait there for her equal's return. The thing is: it didn't make much sense, given their mutual intuition, the other anyway would know nearly straightaway all that happened out there in the walnut grove. Also, they spoke sparingly about the specifics of any particular outing, unlike how it had been at the beginning; from this it can be seen that each on her own never neglected a single detail: the same tone of voice, the same graceful charm: which meant that there wasn't a chance in hell that even by that time the boyfriend suspected there were two rather than one. How could he have?! Only the idle one would make a few terse comments: "Things didn't go so well; you were bored. He talked about pigs, don't deny it." Or, on the contrary: "It was an inspired afternoon, wasn't it?" and the other would nod.

One weighty reason not to go around spying on each other was that even the lowliest of the town's inhabitants were already aware of the glorious romance. They likely drummed up their own hackneyed conclusions, mostly because there's a whole lot of dead time in this town. And here, any courtship is a downright puzzle until finally the date of the wedding can be surmised or is announced; it stops being a problem once the not-so-fair maiden explains to whomever is asking the specific reasons for the glacial pace. But since the sign in the shop read: DO NOT DISTURB . . . RESTRICT YOUR CONVERSATION TO THE BUSINESS AT HAND . . . the Ocampan gossip mill was running at full tilt. Moreover, still pending—and this is conditional—was which of them the man had set his sights on, as well as the glaring doubt about whether that stranger already knew both of them and if he could differentiate between them based on a single feature anywhere. No. Indeed. It was of course better for them to keep those details secret.

And, the final twist: why in the walnut grove, why there, when all couples meet—and always have met—in the town square, the only square in town? This is a very serious issue, in the opinion of many, and it is highly likely that at least one spy observed them from behind some bushes. None of the three, however, noticed any movement or peeping eyes in case there were any nearby; and anyway they weren't going to go farther away—past the nopales or anything like that—just because they'd been seen or heard.

The upshot, alas!: love sprouted, and grew, like ever-searching ivy: inwardly: by necessity: never flagging: a secret force that loses its way because it's all so unfathomable; in the same way, hypocrisy was born: between the twins: how unbecoming!: and although they sensed it, they didn't utter a peep about this dreary development because they wanted to avoid, they thought, a probably foolish confrontation. Their usual kindnesses: everything they had so diligently nurtured to avoid anger between them, now—and this *now* looms quite large—: they no longer cared; they had vaguely fallen in love, like two capricious adolescents, and that's why they were teetering on the verge of hysteria . . . Well, really because there was a subject they couldn't broach between them: the blessed nuptials, the critical future.

The big proposal: which Sunday would it come? To wait: but for how long? . . . It's just that sometimes Oscar, when sitting on one of the tree trunks next to his beloved, would suddenly stare off into the horizon, as if the colors of the afternoon held the key to the tribute he would pay. Tense moments when he'd babble incoherently, and, not daring to mention marriage, would turn to his favorite subject: the weaning of she-goats and the complications that arise from the fattening of swine, as well as his alabastrine desire to one day open, next to any road whatsoever, a huge restaurant for truckers only, serving *carnes adobadas* and fresh tortillas, where there would be a jukebox and a dance floor and some shabby sluts—who would double as grub-slingers—available for pickup.

A great business venture, maybe.

Oscar churned the project over in his mind with a daring that bordered on madness, but his plans didn't include his Constitución, who could, after all, be put in charge of the kitchen; maybe he didn't because he thought that a good wife should stay at home, taking care of her brood.

Frankly, Gloria was not the least bit interested in such blather, but Constitución found it amusing. As for the former: the takeaway from all this was to feel loved by a real man until the day death put an end to the pleasure, to have him always near, to love him with determination, and now she'd had her chance . . . What else could she ask for? Whereas the other was interested in quickly starting a family before she got too old. So, when she studied her boyfriend's features, she sketched in her mind the faces of her children.

These discrepancies, even if conveniently concealed, led to the Gamal sisters becoming a bit rude. A hint of rude, because words never wound as much as deeds, and accordingly, a lack of consideration, or a certain indifference, became more pronounced as the days went by. Shouldering her own plan, each forgot she had an equal, and their similarity slowly became an obstacle: like putty in their conscience; so, in the shop—the first to wake up went early to open. And washing and leaving (quickly dressed) without telling the other—they could work all morning without once looking at each other; at home: remote: at lunch and dinner, each staring at her own meager plate, though still—more to be cynical than urbane—one would make as if to share with her twin her small portion of poached eggs in salsa or her *frijoles charros* or whatever morsel she had; and above all: when it came to outings with their beau, she who was left behind to twiddle her thumbs, also sealed her lips: the idle one, she who was consigned to her bedroom.

Intentionally or not, they slowly became opponents, though despite the magnitude of their jealousy and ingratitude, the knot of their shared lives had not shaken loose.

At bedtime, they were nothing but two ghostly and ataxic monkeys furtively wrapping themselves in sheets and blankets with the falsest possible modesty. And then their dreams, in some ways the same, might have corresponded to their predictions, which each safeguarded as if it were a favorite ornament, safeguarded to avoid wounding her other half. Picturing themselves far away or picturing themselves together, but always with Oscar: which one? On the off chance that he would accept a rather peculiar marriage: with two wives, who are in fact one, so . . .

In a case this convoluted, circumspection held sway. It was time for keen reflection. And since both knew that their hoodwinked boyfriend was an honorable man, in his own way, would that insanity, living with both of them, as reiterations, and in the same bed, be good for him? . . . Everything was still up in the air . . . In the meantime: more of the same: there was such a backlog of work, they hadn't time to think about future rewards. On automatic: and their customers discreetly offered their tact, along with yards of fabric they'd soon come back to collect, sometimes in only a few hours, as perfectly sewn garments: the money: their purpose: which they stashed under a mattress. And the outings and Oscar with his obsessive objective: the huge restaurant that hopefully . . .

As if nothing of any importance was going on, the seamstresses focused anew on what had earned them their reputation. Their image was little by little getting spiffed up, and their productivity spoke volumes of their unrivaled harmony, of a life tethered to a single foundation: exquisite work done quickly. Though if people knew the truth, they'd know that deep down inside simmered nothing but the basest of passions, still controlled, perhaps, by that indissoluble devotion to their age-old sameness.

In the end, a vain contrivance. They were like two excessively celebrated actresses whose eccentricities people find a way to forgive. What would be seen as a defect in anybody else was in them a mere peculiarity. If one of them held hands with her boyfriend on the way to the walnut grove: it was original and that was the end of it. If the other (either one) at some point clung to the walls like a spider, it was because she was watching over her twin and because she didn't know if that stranger was decent or not, and she'd find out by keeping an eye on him and her sister. In short: "You reap what you sow . . . ," or so went the facile adage they'd heard so often wherever they'd been.

But let's now put on our spectacles and peer more closely at their dark reality: they almost never looked at each other: a nascent horror of seeing themselves, like a curse, repeated. Why, after all these years, didn't they look any different, not even when expressing hatred or joy? Why was God so mean as to turn them—and only them—into such a crazy joke? Which meant that, to talk to each other . . . Only every once in a while, maybe because they knew they could change their destinies by again tossing a coin for their beau, and that meant never seeing each other, even hating each other, severing their union: now truly noxious and monstrous. Both mulled this over in the same way and deep down inside, and since their intuition laid bare both of their nasty ambuscades, they were afraid to confront their truths.

But, about that coin toss: they read it in each other's minds, and saw the long threads that would unravel in its wake. Oh, my goodness! Two-headed snakes, talebearers, *maquiscoatl* witches, who while focused on their stitches struggled to know what mortal sin their parents, now cadavers, had passed on to them that they had to pay with their lives. And each reproached herself for not being devout enough, not even to a saint or to the image of any virgin.

They spent horrible days silently sulking and exchanging glances both gloomy and askance.

One night at dinner Constitución finally dared to break the ice. Someone had to speak, so let it be the chatterbox—we could've guessed—and not without a certain amount of trepidation, for she was broaching a thorny subject:

"We still look alike, but maybe our obsession with looking alike is what's holding us back. The thing is . . . Well, you know what I'm talking about! So, for a few weeks now I've been thinking that what has always been a virtue has become a defect that might destroy us."

Gloria, who was washing the dishes, looked her up and down like an inquisitor as if to say: "Okay, now let's see what's in this can of worms." Because she, caught by surprise, wasn't thinking of mentioning the problem. On the contrary, her master plan was to play her cards close until the whole thing blew up, but cruel destiny was saying to them "Here, take that!" and destiny is nothing but a trickster demon. There was, however, no hope, they were so much alike that they could not sequester even their deepest secrets, so she answered stiffly:

"I've been thinking about that, too . . ."

"So, what do you think we should do about it?"

Gloria, hesitating, kept at her task, and after a gray moment of temperance, she answered quietly:

"There are many solutions, but all of them are awful . . ."

"We have to come up with one good one."

"Look, I can't think of anything. What I will confess is that at this stage of the mess we're in, being twins really bothers me. To tell the truth, I believe that we're going to be done for, because we can't keep tricking Oscar; we know full well that rumors spread quickly around here, and in the end, somebody's going to tell him straight out what's going on."

"But, do you think people know that he's going out with both of us? Do you think anyone has noticed?"

"I don't imagine so. I want to think not."

"You're sure optimistic."

"The issue is simple. If what you say were true, one of our customers would have already said something. As you know, the people of Ocampo aren't famous for their discretion. Everybody, even the children, are big blabbermouths; there's always somebody ready to spill the beans, even if it does harm. No, for sure neither Oscar nor anybody else knows about our trick; and what's more: sometimes I think that God or the Devil has arranged everything so that it will stay between the two of us."

Listening in amazement to her sister's fresh deductions: Constitución: still sitting: began to scold her rashly, spewing forth a harangue: "Ssh! Stop it! Get a grip on yourself!" just like a mother who sees her daughter about to pour honey on her beans or sprinkle red-hot chili peppers in her watermelon juice, and again, she shouted at her in a commanding voice:

"Come over here! Sit down! Stop all this nonsense! We have to talk about what's been bothering us and making us so dreary for the past three weeks, and we've got to figure out how to prevent things from happening that we don't want to happen."

Gloria, bewildered, ceased her soaping and rinsing and strode valiantly back to the table. Then, defiantly, she unexpectedly dropped into a chair while bringing the palm of her right hand to her slightly greasy chin, in a show of interest. Disgusting mule! Constitución, however, ignoring this affront, continued:

"The way I see it, our dear boyfriend already suspects that we're up to something fishy, don't think he's so dumb that he doesn't realize that his Constitución is sometimes swapped out for someone who looks just like her, but he plays the fool to avoid a confrontation or maybe just for the fun of it; to tell you the truth, I think he sees this whole thing as a game, and that's why he's never mentioned marriage."

"I'm not so convinced," Gloria said coldly. "If he were a fortune hunter, he'd have suggested we have sexual relations long ago, and he'd have done so with his arms akimbo. Because I don't think that a man of that ilk would accept the monotony of kissing and caressing. It would be way too boring for him. He'd be so horny, he'd always be demanding more."

"Do you really think that he takes us seriously, I mean, takes me seriously?"

"There is something very refined and deep about him: his face glows with the nobility of a rancher but also with firm convictions. No, he's not a playboy, and even if he's never directly mentioned marriage, he insinuates it whenever he describes his plans for the future. Aren't you sick of hearing about his restaurant? You know, he seems like a little kid who wants to fly like a bird . . . I think he wants to convince himself little by little of his love for his sweetheart and that's how he'll summon the courage."

"Well, according to what you're saying, the date is fast approaching when he'll tell one of us that he wants to get married and that he's already saved enough to cover the cost of the wedding, including the wedding dress; and so, if that happens, what'll we say?"

"We'll tell him the truth."

"Oh, no, he'll be so disappointed. He'll feel like he's been tricked in the worst possible way. He'll tell us to get lost, if not something worse. Because: he couldn't face society or his parents, or himself, if he agreed to marry both of us, and the law wouldn't allow it, and even if we forget about marriage, because that's a lot to ask for, even just if he lived with two who are the same. No, we'll be sunk if we tell him the truth."

"So, what do you propose?"

Herein lies the drama, the underbelly of the plot. The

real girlfriend finally lowered her eyes, feeling sly as a fox for having guided the conversation to this convenient (for her) juncture; because this was her chance to reveal her plan: plotted out in her most recent dreams, and here it is: their chitter-chatter had reached a point where their certainties had to be divided in two, because there's nothing else *to* do. That said, if the solution is within reach, some kind of order must be established, and the silence that fell—the conceit—suggested a possibly favorable outcome . . . After a brief pause, Gloria looked up, revealing an almost diabolical expression: without blinking: intense, so shimmery it was spooky, and that look evoked empathy, attentive inquiry, and:

"I've been thinking about what I'm about to say since we were little, and now we'll see what you think . . . Look, the fact that we're identical twins to the *n*th and highest degree fills me with joy on the one hand, and on the other, it doesn't, and this 'doesn't' worries me. Once we said that our likeness was a curse, and I think that God has been punishing us ever since our parents died, it can't be just a fluke that after so many years, we still don't look any different, not even a tiny little bit! I remember when Aunt Soledad brought us the news back in Lamadrid, and I also remember that we were starving to death. She rescued us, comforted us, but she also told us that our parents had been buried in a common grave somewhere near Múzquiz along with the others who'd died in that accident, and the families were supposed to go there one day and claim their bodies. We didn't do that, who knows why, well—naturally! we were just kids, and it would have been too difficult for us, but our aunt never bothered and neither did her husband. But none of that matters. In the end, we're to blame, and that's why the Devil has cursed us, spit on us, our entire lives, yes, the curse is this sameness that now, because of love, is making us suffer."

"Is that really what you think?"

"Yes, it is, so I'm proposing we go to the cemetery in Múzquiz as soon as possible, and we dig up their bodies, or, rather, we go to the authorities in charge to claim them. Though, come to think of it, I imagine that by now their bodies would be almost unrecognizable."

"Are you nuts? How can we ever prove that we're really the daughters of a couple of dead people buried along with a bunch of other dead people? Who's going to believe us after thirty years? More likely, if we do what you suggest, they'll send us straight to the loony bin in Piedras Negras."

"But it's our right, they're our flesh and blood! What if we say that we didn't know till now where they'd been buried?"

"Even so, we'd still need the necessary papers: our birth certificates or something like that, and we don't have anything that proves that we're the daughters of two of the cadavers in the pile."

"And what if the pit no longer exists? What if other families have already claimed their bodies?"

"The fact is, we don't have the paperwork."

"Well, I don't think it's impossible; just going there and making a claim would be enough, because it wouldn't seem weird at all for two people to want two bodies that are buried there in a great big pit, though they might wonder why we would want them, what two living people are going to do with two dead bodies . . . The truth is, sister, I don't see a downside. In any case, it's our only salvation, plain and simple. If what we want is to not look alike anymore, I can't think of a more efficient way to bring that about. And then it's just a matter of burying them here in hallowed ground and bringing them flowers all the time, and the more often we visit their graves, the more our features will change. We have to believe it because that's what's best for us. We can carry their remains in a sack and place them way in the back of the luggage compartment under the bus. First, though, we'd douse them with perfume so the smell of decay doesn't drift up into the bus where the passengers are sitting, or standing, or whatever. You'll see, I'm sure it'll work out. We'll be different!"

"I don't want to. It sounds really ghoulish to me. You should just go by yourself, if you want to."

"No, it'd be better to go together; if our goal is to stop looking alike, we have to both go."

The conversation continued, and continued to be disparaging, insidious, awful. Gloria resisted by raising objection after objection, but she finally ran out and had to give in. She wanted to convince herself that both of their destinies depended on this act. She wanted to believe in it the same way one believes in God and angels who live so very far away, in heaven, and come to visit only once in a while and then only in spirit. But people don't live with doubts, on the contrary: they pray to what's invisible or to some image X; words like *salvation, dissimilarity, success* sounded merely like faith to Gloria, and faith is either abstract or very simple, and on the strength of contrasts, the simple won out. If it was deceptive, well, it couldn't be, because then what would remain?

At this point, Gloria, if only to hear more perfunctory confidences, let slip a question: And then we'll separate?

Well, the answer came later . . . Actually, right away. Yes, for love, that is: depending on the beau . . . New bonds . . . Looking different was not about splitting apart and with one snip of the scissors cutting the old sisterly knot, but rather loosening it, little by little.

A mixture of horror and hope started to seep into their minds, and that went on for weeks.

Weeks of tension in which both of them went with Oscar to the walnut grove as usual and received gifts and kisses and caresses without his mentioning a word about marriage or straight out asking—as they say—for one of their hands.

Unhappy weeks in which they made plans and discussed details, such as: the exact amount of time they would need to go to Múzquiz and get their parents and give them a Christian burial back here. No more than a week so they wouldn't have to cancel any dates with their boyfriend. "It's so complicated." "No, we can arrange everything so that it works out just right." "It seems impossible to do it in six days." In any case: preparing for Sunday, though very fearful of hearing the grand proposal.

But no: everything proceeded peacefully.

And to top it off: every day for weeks now they'd been finding slipped under their door desperate letters from their aunt repeating the same annoying drivel, creeping toward the cynical: written hastily, with letters that were almost Chinese: worse than a doctor's, though at the bottom—after the P.S. appeared this scoundrelly sentence written in all capital letters: GET MARRIED SOON, YOU IDIOTS. Letters they ripped up without even opening: weak rudiments of comfort. Later came the real mess: sublime dalliance. Because: so many baskets overflowing with shreds: the fruit of recurrent jitters: they decided to empty all that trash into the middle of the patio and light an unforgettable bonfire: where: as if it were really a ritual: a bunch of ashes took flight and when they danced in the air, they looked like vague ideas or black butterflies.

What fades away and fades away again: the charm of other days or their concerns.

But the missives kept arriving, like a litany.

Such a cruelly cheerful feeling: daily bonfires, almost at dawn: because there was no other time to do it. Baby butterflies with limber letters rather than colorful patterns!

This was the only chance they had to be idle and fascinated, for all their other lived moments—by night, gliding; by day, always the same—were spent trying to figure out the best way to go dig up their progenitors: calculating how much time it would take if everything went according to plan.

The days also flew by and they failed to reach any agreement, until one night Gloria said:

"Let's decide on a date . . . I propose next Monday. There's a bus that leaves here around six in the morning, that's the one we should take because it arrives in Múzquiz around four in the afternoon, maybe even earlier, if it doesn't stop at every ranch along the way. Then, if you want, we can check into a second- or even a third-class hotel, if there is one, or we can sleep in the seats at the bus station to save money. But really, we can also see this little trip as a vacation, we can stroll around the square and through the streets of the town and buy food from street vendors. Then we can spend all of Tuesday taking care of our business, let's hope one day is enough . . . Then . . ."

"Wait a second, we still haven't picked out and paid for a plot in the cemetery here in Ocampo."

"Oh, that doesn't matter. We can store the sack with their remains in our house for the time being. The important thing is to bring it back . . . How about we put it in the middle of the patio, right where we make our bonfires, maybe that would bring about better results? And what's more, it won't matter if it gets wet if it rains . . ."

Alas, she said it with such aplomb, as if she'd studied this reasoning.

They'd switched roles.

No matter how much they wanted to be different, there was clear symbiosis in their psychological makeup. Hence, she who had at first had reservations—obviously she now wanted to take the lead—removed her mask to shake off any anxiety that would show her to be weak; this one: today she was the sinister sister, who brought things to a head, and they agreed to go on Monday.

However . . .

Sunday arrived. The afternoon. The proud sweetheart all gussied up and waiting in the usual place. The beau—oh, dear!—arrived without the usual gift, and decked out in a suit and tie! in spite of the heat, and hatless to boot! Bah . . . Hair slicked back with thick brilliantine, in an impeccable and old-fashioned do. Constitución—it was her turn—greeted him with a peck on the cheek: such delightful proximity! The nectar of love, about to be enveloped. A rancher who changes clothes for no apparent reason: excessive amicability, and: close-up smiles: what a penetrating woodland perfume! Might something special be brewing?

Yes.

In the meantime they held hands: and: slowly strolling: a gentle breeze: toward the walnut grove: as if happily on their way to paradise, down a long ramp. Along the way, and accompanying many glances, there was a laconic exchange of words:

"I love you." "So do I." "I adore you." "Me, too" . . . Who, me? And other honeyed magmas.

The color of evening was yellow—our lovers finally sitting on one of many fallen tree trunks—and spread itself across the sown fields: whence came the augury of dissipation. Oscar pulled out of his jacket's inside pocket a card on which was written in rather stylized lettering the name of his sweetheart, and below, in purple, the splendid drawing of a flower. It had meaning, the hint of a riddle. If flower, then Constitución . . . The petals were alive, did each hold a . . . secret? And though her blushing spoke volumes, she expressed her gratitude like this:

"I love your gift, it's so imaginative."

"Please, open it."

The grateful woman did so and discovered these words: *My love, would you agree to marry your very own Oscar? I am asking for your hand in marriage, for you to stand beside me at the altar. Do you accept?* She felt an unusual fire inside her, and wanted to say *yes!* but her sister, her parents' remains, the lie, the truth.

"What's your answer?" Oscar asked.

Constitución didn't know, or . . . Well. Though . . . She gazed at him lovingly, and there were sparks in her eyes and blushes on her cheeks. Her mouth-heart longed to speak, but no, no impulsiveness now. How unfortunate that this bombshell dropped precisely the day before they were taking off for Múzquiz, or rather, there was still a week to go before she'd be different from her twin. Oh, dear! But she gave an answer because her suitor required one:

"I've been waiting for you to ask, and I'm proud and excited that you would want me to be your wife . . . Right now, I won't say yes or no, but I'll answer you in my own way."

And she embraces him and, what nerve!: she gives him a kiss, and it went on and on. Mouths open, tongues and bliss, and that forty-something-year-old inevitably shed a tear, which wet the cheek of her beau, who stopped in the act when he felt it.

"Why are you crying, my love?"

"Because what you have asked me is incredible, I'm thrilled. I'm crying from happiness."

"Hey, that's no way to celebrate!"

"Oh, forgive me."

"No, it's okay. Let me wipe away those tears."

Oscar pulled out of his suit a foreign-colored handkerchief: pellucid yellow, and proceeded to wipe her off from top to bottom. It was quick, it was very gentle.

"So, you accept?"

"You can interpret it yourself. You're a smart man."

"Yes, yes, yes! You've made me so happy! I love you!"

"Just kiss me."

And they kept blissfully kissing each other. Caresses, turbulence, and currents that swell to accommodate this business of longing and that demand that hands pass along bodies, to know oneself as one, in two, in one: finally; hands that want to cling to the entirety of the pleasure. Legs and breasts. Robust rancher arms. Hidden florets and figurations, though placing grand romanticism above and beyond all: even to the extent of grasping at robust odors, she, in particular, because when her wandering hand playfully touched his hair, it got drenched in brilliantine, which she then proceeded to smear, perhaps unintentionally, all over his dark green suit.

She palmed off, for the moment, any evident return to her ancient agreement with her sister. That similitude, so prone to ripping apart, was at the mercy of a definitive *yes*. But their incomparable shared history, their orphanhood, their work: legacies that made their diligence the center of their life, that couldn't be erased with a single stroke, but rather: the hope remained, today more than ever, of bringing home their dead parents. That specific and conceptual goal that just might make them prettier. And now, while she kissed the man with desperation, she thought of a grave problem that had not yet occurred to either of them. That is: connecting the dots, the *yes* started to teeter, because if they were really going to change, who would change first? And then Oscar might feel cheated, indirectly: if, let's say, Constitución's delicious mouth or brown eyes were to change. Here's something they had not, unfortunately, foreseen.

So it was, between kisses and gropings, their trip to Múzquiz fell apart. Let's remember that it was the now really lucky one who'd had the idea of bringing back their dead in order to start looking different; as opposed to Gloria, who'd demurred from the get-go because the whole thing had seemed insane to her, and who'd agreed only with the belief, somewhat incidental, that she'd then have a destiny different from her other half. So, more concretely, it wasn't difficult to get Constitución to see their plan in a slightly different light, though it was bitter. And the idea that as a result of that sinister act, both of them would no longer be what they had been, come now! This had never been anything more than an illusion.

For a moment the chosen one had a glimpse of something pathetic, because individualism, which is nothing but amorphous vanity, can sometimes gain momentum, and here was a way to make that happen. She realized how easy it would be to run off with her Oscar, because in this part of the country, eloping is all the rage in order to avoid the expense of a wedding, and it is smiled upon by fathers, grandfathers, and sons, among the educated classes or not, and for this very reason, if she proposed it, her beau would most surely agree, and then she could patch things up later; but she changed her mind, because leaving her twin in the lurch was as dishonest as never telling her suitor that there were two, rather than one, he was wooing.

Evening came. And the good-bye, hopeful with good reason, and the magically charged words: "So, you will have me?"

"You can interpret it yourself, as I said. But we'll see each other next Sunday." "You make me so happy, my love." "Well, I'm not at all sad myself." Fine indelible forebodings. As was customary, and expected, Oscar accompanied her right to the door of the shop, where he met her week after week, not to the house, because, as she'd told him long before, if he took her there people might think he snuck or crept in where it wasn't at all proper for him to be: once there, quickly strip and smugly proceed with that filthy extramarital business, and that's why, as the saying goes: "Never do a good thing that others might judge to be bad." This was a philosophy one had to respect.

There, at the aforementioned spot, they bid each other

farewell, and once the outline of the beau's figure—with that thin thread of a shadow trailing behind—had vanished, she closed her eyes.

To suffer forevermore merely because of their cruel yoke, when she, the chosen one, would easily be on the upswing of any outcome? She wasn't about to let that go, seeing as how it was now possible to arrange things to her liking. In the end, she would find an excuse that would satisfy three people who love and understand one another. So, standing there like a statue with a sullen face, Constitución suddenly changed, as if struck by a bolt of lightning that would lead her to her house with a bulb lit above her head, and she took off running to see her other half and bring her the news. A live wire: her hair standing on end. Her high heels clicking the pavement. That unique excitement of knowing that she was the only chosen one, the one God or maybe even the Devil had chosen at the most decisive moment, hence with the courage to confront her twin in the heat of the moment. To tell her, with a mixture of ingenuity and well-oiled wit, what she had been telling herself so fearlessly ever since her beau had disappeared in the distance.

Lots of light in the house and, whoosh!: the door swung open to let in the half-crazed real sweetheart, babbling all manner of nonsense. But she got a grip on herself, because: all those beneficial changes, in spite of being radical, couldn't just be blurted out, for Gloria, who was sorting beans at the table, was listening to a whip-like polka at high volume, nothing more nor less than a song by Los Relámpagos, the Lightning Bolts, with a *tololoche* solo and an accordion wailing in semitones in the background. Her sister was in ecstasy—such contorted and inspired tangles!—too bad, the dunce would have to turn it down; at a sign, she complied, only to hear:

"We can't possibly go to Múzquiz!"

Then the same old explanation. One step at a time, all the deficiencies that did not and never would do anything but cause horrible harm, in particular when their three or four objectives came up against this reasoning: which of the two would change first?, because miracles, no matter how strange, aren't wrought with a plethora of detail but rather in a general kind of way. It was feasible that Gloria, busy much of the afternoon with her bean sorting and the delightful sounds of her borderland polkas, had already thought of that, so she showed no particular concern. Nor was it a victory for her, simply a showdown.

Therefore, and sadly, the remains of their parents no longer mattered.

The issue unmoored . . .

Next, the petition, in short, the marriage, what both had been expecting but not that Sunday, and here's the surprise:

"I didn't tell Oscar yes or no, I left it up in the air, or rather I told him to interpret it himself, though I did kiss him and hug him as a kind of answer. The thing is, I think I'll say yes: I want to get married, and soon."

"What about me?"

"Well, I don't know what to think . . . I gave you the opportunity to have a little fun, and that was a big gift for you, but it was my good luck to have met him first, and my double good luck that he asked for my hand in marriage. Isn't it exciting? . . . If you really care about me, you'll understand that this is a great opportunity for me."

The collapse of the other, who nonetheless stood up

bravely without making a fuss or expressing any distress, and off she went, straightaway—even if extremely slowly—to her bedroom to lie down and think about specific courses of action and the consequences thereof. After such a lashing, best would have been to grope her way to bed, but that's not what she did; her step was steady, and as the light there was on, she switched it off and lit a candle, which they both did often when they were at a loss. All of these actions were scrupulously observed by the now truly victorious twin, who didn't move, aside from her head, which was indiscreet. As it happened, there were no tears.

Beans: the good and the bad shouldn't mingle once they've been sorted. Constitución analyzed timorously. Hardships, plans, the first cause serious shrinkage whereas the second become inflexible and tend to win out. Which of the two piles on the table contained the most beans? Each bean would have to be counted—requisite patience—because they looked the same at a glance, but if the difference was minimal, small concessions would have to be made, because: a feeling can carry as much weight as a law: or vice versa, and this made the real sweetheart set about counting raucously and out loud the pile that was still full of grit. As soon as her sister, lying in bed in the next room, heard *one, two, three, four,* she called out in a commanding voice, whereat this one rose immediately and went running smugly to the other: who was already standing up: the now definite leftover distressingly backlit by a lively flame.

"I understand you well enough. You have the right, and I know full well that it's silly to play childish games when it comes to marriage. I'm going to leave this house forever, yes, that's what I think is best. I promise you'll never see me again because I'm planning to go far away. I admit, I might one day feel like seeing you, but I'll be so far away, it won't even be possible. Forgetting will be difficult because it's like a ghost that wends its way in and out of our thoughts at will, but time is wiser because it contains your death and my own. On the other hand, don't think my going who-knows-where is just some passing whim; I'm doing it because I know that my presence would only complicate your relationship with Oscar, and then he'd wonder which of the two was truly his wife. I don't want to be in the way, that's not what I was born for . . . And since there have never been any stupid accusations or tit-for-tats between us, I've decided that you should keep everything, that is, the shop, the house, the furniture, everything except our savings, which I'll take. It's the best way to make us square. Don't you think?"

"Yes, I agree."

"So, I'll leave tomorrow."

"Fine by me."

For the moment there was nothing left for them to do but switch off the lights and get into bed and good night. Happiness? Anguish? Irreproachable maturity?

Darkness, interior ruminations, a lively flame: left lit: by both: possibly for very different reasons. And it trembles if the sighs of nearby words bend it and make it flicker. If it spoke: what would it say? To merely illuminate such a confined space expresses enough. It is perpetual resolve that speaks by blinking, and only rarely, if ever, lets itself be caressed, and abruptly returns to its own shape when left alone: then remains, immaculate.

Because here the silences crown that flame as queen: a

lone reality surrounded by myriad mysteries, lively plenitude requiring a fixed gaze, yes, Constitución's, who has yet to fall asleep, whereas the other is already deliriously dreaming.

Dream and gaze are leisure and faith. Throbbing terror, anticipation that conjures paths and precipices. Everything is halved. It's comforting to look back, whereas the future might be diffuse. And those eyes wide open: what hopes do they hold? Desires lasting but an instant, and under the circumstances merely melancholic: what began then ended: that sameness that can be no longer because the Devil has come to settle down right smack in between them, disguised as a magician, and how to get rid of him now? With words? The other half leaving forever and the Devil playing the role of the one who lost: is that a solution? Though if one half chooses what best suits her, any imprecision becomes whimsy or destiny; to seek wholeness, to wish to preserve it, maybe that's just faith that hasn't anywhere much to go.

Or does it?

Constitución needed light. *Yes* and *no* were both dissembling.

Because the flame—given to dalliance—flickers when it feels that someone within its illuminated sphere cannot find a simple and conclusive idea.

At that moment, however, the fiancée wanted to go to the dining room, switch on the electric light, and serenely count beans: the good and the bad: how many?: in order to likewise sort her thoughts, but just as she was about to begin, she stopped. Convinced the act was futile, she understood that right there in her bed, in the semidarkness, she could find the remedy that would allow her to sleep like her other half. In other words, she didn't need beans to see sense, or light, or any damn thing at all.

Constitución decided to think about her fiancé, Oscar, her rancher and dreamer. His conversation. His life: like a predictably preterit respite: happiness admitted for stretches and much-too-subtle dissatisfaction. His spirit of struggle limited to surveying what is closest at hand. In him, there's no emancipation, no adventure. Would the man be worth it? She cannot imagine how the weaning of she-goats and the raising of swine can so fully occupy his lucid thoughts. In the meantime, the lively flame seemed to smile, as if to ask sardonically: and what about you? Your sewing: what's that? Your identity: what can it presume?

Such well-delineated lives, where longing is neither an ascent nor an earthly fire. Lives in purgatory, which are, after all, what others think they are, and if that makes sense then let that sense continue, culminate, so many lives draw together and so many move apart. To seek similarities: what for?, there are loads of them in some way or other.

And the fiancée thought about life with her future husband, who, for example, during all those Sunday outings had never once asked her how her business was going. Only at the very beginning were there a few questions, but this was just to get a general overview; the man certainly would never agree to let her work on her own or God forbid earn more than he! Horrors! Cruel humiliation! On the contrary, soon, indeed, he would reveal his own sinister plan, pull the rug out from under his splendid spouse by selling off her dressmaking business and using the profits to buy his truck or maybe that restaurant of his, serving *tacos de carnitas:* smack in the middle of the desert, though next to some highway; that's right: where his wife, joined to him in holy matrimony, would oversee a bevy of girls. A life of despairingly small chores. A life up to her neck in soups and reheatings, in cooking and cleaning up messes. A life in an apron. And the man: lord and master, who will strut his stuff and stroke his long black mustache, black like her image of him in profile or looking at him head-on. Not to mention the children and the family hearth. Would this be the reward for kisses that would continue for who knows how much longer?

No!

Wide awake, the fiancée thought it better to snuff out that light, that despicable candle, whose flame was a mockery, a terrifying and mendacious burn. She rises swiftly—it was midnight or even later—and angrily blows it out.

Darkness and the end.

"Gloria! Gloria, for heaven's sake, are you still asleep?"

"What? . . . Huh?" answered drowsily she who was dreaming of sibylline locales in savory company.

"Wake up, woman! I want to turn this thing around."

"Ahh . . . At this hour? . . . Ugh! Why don't you tell me about it tomorrow?"

"It's urgent, you have to hear me out!"

The other half, the good one, shifted sleepily in bed, pulled up the blanket, then said:

"Tomorrow is Monday . . . Mmm . . . We'll talk tomorrow."

"I'd rather talk now than work tomorrow."

"Oh! . . . I was having such a lovely dream . . . Don't ruin it for me . . . Mmm . . . bye-bye!"

There was nothing for the wide-awake one to do but

go and switch on the bedroom light, but she didn't stop there, she poked her twin in the ribs, though playfully, until Gloria finally rubbed her eyes and sat up in bed.

"Let's celebrate!"

"Celebrate what?"

"Do you remember that a long time ago we agreed that what was yours was mine and vice versa, that our sameness must be safeguarded?"

"Yes . . . How could I forget what keeps us together?"

"Oh, please, don't you see, I regret trying to break our bond."

Gloria stood up without saying a word, then walked to the bathroom to wash her face and quickly comb her hair. She returned, still half asleep, mumbling under her breath, she also adept at non sequiturs.

"It's past one, isn't it?"

"I don't know, I have no interest in looking at a watch."

"Aren't you cold?"

"No, and I don't plan to be . . . But tell me: what's wrong with you?"

"How can you ask? You forced me to wake up."

"Forgive me, my darling sister! But . . . the wedding . . . "

"I know what you're going to say."

"What I'm going to say is that there isn't going to be any wedding . . . "

"What?"

And with this "what?" she upended the foolish promise of a rosy future that only ever belonged to the realm of the imagination, to the many-flavored kisses that sublimate in order to distort, and to those soft beginnings that gradually harden. Because in the long run, love would cease to be what dreams dictate and turn instead into insipid bread, intrepid monotony, and in the end and forevermore: subjugated love.

The natural ease of recent days would anyway peter out all on its own, because the effusive man, once satisfied and settled down, would set aside the maelstrom of affection to make room for more pressing concerns of money and work, of hardships and obligations, such as: the goats hanging from the roof grating, and the pigs, too: the stakebed truck, the huge restaurant, and then love would become inferred. In fact, and here's the worst part: it would no longer be possible to sew: to consider it a business: good heavens, no! because it would be unbecoming for the so-called better halves to compete with each other.

Love with a man of his ilk would at first be cheerfully single-minded and at last, the same old servitude . . .

No!

An about-face!

While her twin was explaining: Gloria shuddered, but not from emotion: from disbelief; she had already been planning in her now grubby mind an ironic outcome, a tremendous hoax: engulfing and refined, but she waited till the other had used up all her reserves and been rendered too weak to make a single insipid remark about salvaging their broken harmony: that ancient unity—and what a unity it was—tainted by the Devil.

Constitución, weary of disclosing her motives, was trying to be very prudent when she said:

"I hope you agree that we should go on living as we did before . . . "

Gloria broke out laughing and said sarcastically:

"No way, not that!"

"What? . . . You don't . . . ? Why not?"

"Of course I do, woman! but let it be said that with ranchers we never shall wed."

"Never? . . . Well, I suppose you're right."

"Only with Prince Charmings."

"Where do they come from? Where are they?"

"Seems they do exist . . . No, they couldn't."

Magnificent and similar roars of laughter erupted under the electric light—in the small hours of the morning—which they both decided to switch off so they could light candles: the usual toast?

Of course! To a sensible solution! To pure—and miraculous—joy!

Instant recovery by cleansing with alcohol the toxic sludge they'd been carrying around inside their souls. They looked eagerly for the Club 45, but, bad luck, there wasn't a single drop left, they'd polished it off the last time, when they'd brutishly agreed to share the rancher: that delirious drunken bout with bloodshot oculi; and at that time of night, no way, they'd never find even grain alcohol; but, wait, they had bottles of perfume in the bathroom: dense effluvia and aromatic substances made of crushed flowers and eucalyptus bark, yes, that's it, why not!?, all they had to do was dilute it a little, and they'd get tipsy just imagining what was in store for them, though:

"No, it'll be bad for us. Our happiness doesn't have to come so cheap."

"That's fine, I'm okay with just putting on some music and dancing."

So it was—pipe dreams, half-closed eyes to match the flame-lit ambience, like two mischievous girls, they took out every candle they could find, and—*cumbia* music: weaving and heaving: one record after another—both of them, winged, trying new steps, which didn't work so well because the rhythm was different, until they collapsed at dawn, and lying there on the floor they planned next Sunday's final episode. In essence, it consisted of telling the doomed man the truth, and when the supposed fiancée remembered how he was dressed when he asked for her hand: she burst out laughing and prodded the other to do likewise. The truth, above all, in a single stroke—that they were two rather than one—but with a particular twist . . . It didn't take them long to figure out how, and once they had, they fell asleep where they lay . . . As we shall soon see, they didn't need to make plans, because . . .

/

The bus arrived in Ocampo at a quarter to three in the afternoon: a little earlier than usual: on Sundays, it normally arrives at three on the dot. The beau was riding up front: perfumed to a noxious extent and decked out in green, with his hair parted down the middle, to perfection: in his own way, he called attention to himself. He descended like a king, flowers in his left hand and a gift decorated with a curlicue bow with spikes in his right. He looked from side to side with his bullish eyes as if to say to anyone who dared deride him: "I bet you wish you were me." Today, his ambition: to walk through those dusty streets as if treading on clouds, and yes: he briefly gave that impression, even if despite himself: he couldn't hide his cowboy stride no matter how he spiffed himself up.

Usually, to fortify himself, he had a couple of sodas at a small grocery store, whose owner he knew and who, without being too forthcoming, always conveyed a warm welcome. This time was different:

"Welcome! You look so elegant today. What a surprise."

"Thanks a lot."

Without waiting for his customer to order, the chubby grocer placed two grape sodas on the counter.

"Why the suit, if I may be so bold as to ask?"

"I'm going to wed a local belle. You must know her, none other than Constitución Gamal, the seamstress. Anyway, just to be clear, we're not getting married today, even though that'd be my preference, no, I've still got to bide my time, chew on my cud for a stretch, that is, what I mean is, there'll be no wedding for several months . . . The important thing is, she gave me her word last week, and today is a special day for the two of us . . . There was, you know, a verbal commitment." The perfumed man took a huge gulp of his soda and continued enthusiastically. "We've been courting for some time now, a little over a year, and to be perfectly frank with you, it was mighty hard for me to decide to ask for her hand, well, you know how it is, you have to figure out the best way to win her over. That's why I went all the way to Monterrey to buy this suit. I want my woman to see me at my very best. Maybe next week I won't wear it, because with all this dust it'll get dirty."

"Did you say it was Constitución?"

"That's right, the one and only. Why do you ask?"

"Well, it's just that between the twins, I never can tell which one is which."

"What? What are you talking about?"

"What, didn't you know that Constitución has an identical twin?"

"No! She never told me that."

"You don't say! . . . There are two, exactly the same."

"Really?"

"Cross my heart. And I'm telling you, everybody around here, no matter how hard we try, we still can't tell them apart."

Oscar, speechless, downed his soda in one gulp, then started coughing. Apparently, he couldn't believe his ears. The initial surprise over, and gulping down air while shutting his nostrils—he used all the fingers on his left hand—as a cure, he looked at his watch: it was still early. In the meantime, the instructive grocer saw how upset Oscar was—he went over to the door to look outside at what was going on, then not: what good did it do? No, not at the roof, either (whence he returned with tottering steps): what about that thatch? The walls, even less: cracked and peeling, or the gift (for the moment: absurd) or the bunch of flowers that he'd left on the counter; or those disgusting cans, one still full, and the other now empty, dripping only with saliva. The grocer had no option but to close his eyes for a moment so his thoughts could settle—and feel pangs of compunction and try to find another angle: "Poor man, and there I went: really sticking my foot in it!"—whereat with a sorrowful voice that seemed to come from elsewhere, he gently uttered these words:

"I'm really surprised she didn't tell you."

How could Oscar possibly reply? He again consulted his watch. About thirty minutes before he would see his beloved, who . . . Yes, a sinister idea crossed his mind: that at some point his beloved could have been the other: and he unaware of the deception . . . No! Impossible! His fiancée would never do such a vile thing, and it was wrong for him to even toy with the idea. What folly! He knocked on wood, finally: the counter's: which made the disagreeable shopkeeper prick up his ears, but anyway that dump of a store was beginning to get on our beau's nerves.

"How much do I owe you?"

"Just two pesos."

He paid and rushed out, as if in a hurry to collect his inheritance, or something worse, because he'd mussed his hair while scratching his pompadour parted right down the middle, all because of the unnerving as well as pithy nature of the information he'd heard. He left without saying good-bye and, in addition, without taking the flowers or the gift. He chose to ignore the shouts of the grocer behind him: "Forgive me, sir, I didn't know you didn't know . . ." Then, in a lower voice, almost braying: "Look, they must have just forgotten . . . !" Wretched wind, and street festivities: people who stepped out every Sunday: and whistles: anonymous, and he: like an automaton, looking constantly at his watch as he walked, though not toward the shop, but rather . . . Alas, it would be a newfound pleasure to sit for a few moments on one of the benches in the town square and observe the comings and goings, but calming himself down, trying to see his fiancée's harsh reserve in a positive light.

Why?

He held on to tender hope. Her motives could not be that wicked, that perverse. He sat down without combing his hair—amid the chirping voices of the many passersby: there, as was said, by his own free will: distracted, sullen, but with just enough time to buoy up his illusions, set them on a favorable course: this wasn't difficult though it was somewhat self-deceptive.

Maybe his fiancée—this is how he chose to understand it—had failed to mention that she had a twin sister out of fear of disappointing him, because for him to see two who are the same could create a dilemma as daft as it would be marvelous. To have and to love, magically, two identical sweethearts, and to not be able to marry either because he wouldn't know who the real one was.

This was the reason for her great reserve, but: there was so much racket, he finally got distracted. He looked at the young and beautiful women passing jauntily by and tossing flirtatious smiles his way. Babes everywhere! But his love had alighted. Constitución, splendid and primed, waiting to stand beside him at the altar. Constitución, there, at the door as usual . . . And the beau consulted his watch one last time: ten minutes to four, so now he'd have to rush.

He stood up, ran his fingers through his hair, and started walking. He had the bad habit or the good fortune of always being punctual, even to a perverse extent, especially when it came to matters of love, and this time, well, don't even mention it.

Once he was on his way, he remembered the flowers, and the gift—a handkerchief with little drawings of red hearts—: which he'd stupidly left at the grocer's, what with his plight, his dazed state had led him here: where he needed to be to collect himself, and there was no time to return for his forgotten offerings. What a pity! But now, and focusing on restraint, he could not put aside the most obvious question. His fiancée would have to respond without ifs, ands, or buts about her sister, her twin, the one at least other people confused her with.

As he approached his destination, he saw two women standing at the door, though they still appeared blurry in the evening glare. Now facing the horror, he, too, stopped in his tracks. His eyes alone, switching back and forth, saw two women rather than one, or two sweethearts that were a dreadful optical illusion. The well-groomed man was rendered speechless, for he saw the truth of what moments before the grocer had revealed. Bloodcurdling copies!, in front of him. The nerve! Why was the secret kept from him till now? Because of his proposal? What he'd thought in the square was now visible, the sister who is not and who is, and, which one was which? So he asked with drab diffidence:

"Who is Constitución?"

"That would be me," said one.

"Not so, I'm Constitución."

"Lies! You wish you were, but I'm the real one."

"Don't start in with your jokes. I am Oscar's fiancée."

"But last week he proposed to me."

"Anyway, he asked both of us."

"Don't you get it? He asked me."

"That's what you think, but I'm the one he asked."

And there they were, rattling on and on to each other, throwing poisoned darts back and forth, while Dapper Dan turned ashen with anticipation and fear. Their coarse barbs nurtured his silence, his face turned more green than yellow, then red, as they continued with their: "That's a lie, you are not." "I'm Constitución." "My God, you are such a liar." And when his choler had reached its peak: his pallor turned purplish, like an overripe fig that bursts when it falls from the tree:

"Enough! . . . You're disgusting. You pair of old hags!"

And Oscar turned on his heels and stomped away in a huff, clenching his fists, and he still heard behind him the twins' pitiless giggles. He tried to understand the hoax or the rejection as an awkward business venture gone bad. He happened to hear a question, who knows if caustic or hopeful:

"But you'll come next Sunday, won't you?"

A paradox if ever there was one! but for him: to turn and look back meant to see himself petrified in memory, or rather: to see in a trance all that's twisted turned to salt: the saltiness of love set adrift, though the man was pretty darn tough, being a real rancher and all, despite the suit. What a mistake it would be to turn around! Not even tears made sense, and getting drunk in order to cry his eyes out, even less. Nor was it the right moment to let out a self-congratulatory whoop for having escaped the clutches of that traitorous pair. The good part was the opposite and absolutely cold-blooded: he could now say to himself: "The fight was well fought, but was for naught." Yes, a range of inferences would restore his precious feelings, which were already beginning to point in new directions. And his figure was shrinking, his ridiculed figure, while behind him, the two watched him depart, feeling somehow or other—now that they'd had their fun—a certain pity, especially the real sweetheart, who, driven perhaps by perfidy or sentimentality, took two steps forward, as if still seeking some kind of communion. But no, he kept walking away: a fluke: as he'd come. Constitución trembled: a sigh escaped her and opened a path through the clouds, then thundered beyond . . . Gloria took her arm and pulled gently, as if with a restrained caress.

"Please, dear sister, stop watching. Let's go home."

/

The usual: from then on: split down the middle, bound together by loyalties that reject the nectars and passions offered by a choir of voices that don't project very far. The universe, theirs from now on, might just as well be reduced to the stitching of seams whenever the scissors makes as straight a cut as possible. The thread is what moves forward and in the end holds the pieces together. All threads are proxies and break haphazardly or on a whim. It's worth going back and forth because then somehow a plait is made, edges are wedded, new beginnings forged, the centers are set on fire, and it is one in two or two by now in one. To toil on the back of similitude, of simultaneity. Interior toil that might be a portrayal—probably wanting but felicitous nonetheless—whose subsequent effect would be to create something radiant and unique out of things and thoughts, and perhaps as a bonus: with a double meaning that insinuates still others.

Along with that: daily sisterhood, sewing, the mirror: hidden vanities invented in silence in order to be intentionally expressed, thus to live believing that they vanish and that to affirm them brings a truce that lasts from one minute to the next. We are two peas in a pod—they would later say—that want to be one. Hence, to continue to dress the same was already a boon, the makeup, too, the same haircut, and the same understanding. And if—moving forward to a few months hence—one of the two had an urge to go to Múzquiz out of a moment of vain faith in gradual differentiation, she'd quickly desist, or rather: the topic no longer mattered.

Also: whenever Constitución remembered Oscar, his huge restaurant, the weaning of she-goats, the fattening of swine, the lingering kisses there in the walnut grove, she would suddenly feel nostalgic and go look for that scrap of paper—the one she secretly stashed in one place after another and on which was written his address: the one in Ciudad Frontera. She did this secretly to avoid problems with her sister . . . Bah, in any case it never was more than an ephemeral game that flamed up and fizzled out like a dud . . . Then came a bitter day when she wanted to completely erase all the yesterdays. She took the blessed scrap of paper and, standing precisely in the spot where they had once burned those petulant letters from their aunt, lit a match to it. The address took flight: a warm and passing breeze, no longer worth even a peek.

Speaking of their aunt: in the last few months, no letters had come: nothing, not even one. As if the aforementioned had died, or as if she had no chance to write from heaven.

Looking back, it all boiled down to an auspicious sign that they should again come to terms with being twins who crawl into their shell.

What they'd always been: the passion to be one that never fully is: two, here, so many things. Fusion refashioned.

To dance, to laugh, and, to get drunk: why not? Perchance, to sing: music and labyrinths! . . . Moreover, the real: greeting their customers, then cheerfully dispatching them. Right? But the shop needed spiffing up. Decorations? What kind? In the meantime: whitewash the walls, cover them with doohickeys and photos of nearby locales they snapped with their camera: Sunday outings. And the famous sign . . . RESTRICT YOUR CONVERSATION TO THE BUSINESS AT HAND . . . , once and for all take it down and open themselves up to others, give themselves over more fully to the fabrications that come and go day in and day out; but once they did that, there was suddenly someone who boldly asked one of them point blank:

"Hey, what about that boyfriend I don't know which one of you had? Where is he, what happened to him? Because . . . Nobody in town has seen him again."

"Oh, don't even ask . . . It's too painful . . . He was killed a few months ago on a bus in the north. A horrible accident, very close to Múzquiz," one of them said.

"Oh, I'm so sorry, I'm sorry for even asking; thing is, I didn't know, and to tell the truth, I don't think anybody in town does . . . Poor you . . . As far as I understood it, you were going to get married, weren't you? . . . Well, my heart goes out to you. But, if I'd known sooner, I would have brought flowers."

Death is a good excuse: a good dodge: marvelous lie or harsh reality . . . Otherwise, everything the same: putting pieces together with the same zeal: tendrils of perfectionism. Tailoring and dressmaking to the point of shuddering, like pretending to live in the ambiguous present believing they are one: morning, noon, and night: a circle: vicious or not: that still tries to spin: just because: however possible: as time goes by.

ALSO IN SPEAKING TIGER INTERNATIONAL FICTION

Vengeance Is Mine, All Others Pay Cash | Eka Kurniawan, translated from the Bahasa by Annie Tucker

Vampire in Love: Stories | Enrique Vila-Matas, translated from the Spanish by Margaret Jull Costa

Amba-The Question of Red: A Novel | Laksmi Pamuntjak

Istanbul Istanbul: A Novel | Burhan Sönmez, translated from the Turkish by Ümit Hussein

Man Tiger: Stories | Eka Kurniawan, translated from the Bahasa by Labodalih Sembiring

One Last Drink at Guapa | Saleem Haddad

Tram 83 | Fiston Mwanza Mujila, translated from the French by Roland Glasser

The Yard | Aliyyah Eniath

Tales of the Metric System | Imraan Coovadia

Beauty Is a Wound | Eka Kurniawan, translated from the Bahasa by Annie Tucker

The Devil Is a Black Dog: Stories of War and Revolution from the Middle East and Beyond | Sándor Jászberényi, translated from the Hungarian by M. Henderson Ellis

Uncertain Light | Marion Molteno

The Art of Hearing Heartbeats | Jan-Philipp Sendker, translated from the German by Kevin Wiliarty